Country Club!!!

by

Robert B. Pile

DORRANCE PUBLISHING CO., INC.
PITTSBURGH, PENNSYLVANIA 15222

ISBN # 0-8059-4513-X
Printed in the United States of America

First Printing

For information or to order additional books, please write:
Dorrance Publishing Co., Inc.
643 Smithfield Street
Pittsburgh, Pennsylvania 15222
U.S.A.

Other books by Robert B. Pile

Letters from a French Windmill

Panic in the Morning Mail

Crisis Every 15 Minutes

For the Love of Rose

The Water Walkers

Top Entrepreneurs and their Businesses

Top Women Business Leaders

Contents

Prologue

The golf and country club of today is vastly different from the traditional clubs founded in the U.S. at the turn of the century. Those clubs, mostly in the Eastern part of our country, were golf clubs in the purest sense. They were built as a kind of adjunct to a golf course, the golf course being the important part of the total. Clubhouses were traditional in appearance but almost 100 percent utilitarian, existing primarily as a place where a member could change into golf clothing. There was food available, but nothing particularly fancy came out of what were mostly meager kitchens. Membership in most clubs was male. In most early clubs, women were simply not part of the scene. A golf club was a place for male golfers, period.

The manager of a club in those days was a man not necessarily trained or educated for the job, mostly someone who could keep the books and keep the physical facility neat and tidy. Golf professionals, as is well-known, were looked on as second-class citizens, being holed up in what was usually a small building near the first tee. They seldom went into the clubhouse itself and never went out on the golf course. Their primary job was to see that the members had a good golf course to play, caddies available on request, and play over the eighteen holes would be brisk. The club manager and the club pro were paid very little. The pro could make a few dollars giving lessons. The manager had no such perks. Most clubs had a custodian of some sort, a generalist who could fix things that had to be fixed.

In many early golf clubs, there was usually one man, or perhaps two or three, who had started the club, as often as not with their own money. Their love of golf was the motivator, and their desire for like male companionship was also a strong factor. The golf club of those days was, to use a cliché, a bastion of like-minded males.

Over a period of many years, the golf club slowly changed. Today, a golf club is no longer a place only for golf. It is now, in the full meaning of the word, a "country club." It is a place for families. It must serve first-class food morning, noon and night. It is as much a place for wives as it is for husbands. It is a place for entire families, for teenagers and for small children. It will have a swimming pool, tennis courts, play areas, and various internal facilities for all kinds of entertaining, both formal and informal.

The golf professional of today runs a big-time operation. Not only is he welcome in the clubhouse, he is also expected to play golf with the members. He gives lessons but also has a full-time staff of younger pros to assist him. He's well-paid and runs an up-to-date retail shop for golf equipment and apparel.

The club manager is today a fully trained professional manager, skilled in people resources, in food and beverage management. He must be at once a warm and diplomatic kind of club host, and at the same time a person who can execute club policy and run a very tight ship. At any given time, the club manager may be liked and respected by perhaps half of the total membership. A small percentage of the membership will actively dislike him, and the rest don't really care one way or the other. All they want is good food, good service, and facilities to satisfy their need for sociability and entertaining. A modern country club will have, on a regular basis, wedding receptions, banquets of all kinds and parties of various themes throughout the year. The manager of the modern golf and country club, no matter how good he is, walks constantly on fragile turf. At any time he may be no more than one minor wrong move away from being terminated. The job of a club manager historically runs about five to six years.

The manager runs the club at the dictate of the club board and club officers. Most clubs are run by committees, each with its own special and distinct responsibilities. There will be a grounds committee in charge of the golf course. A house committee in charge of the clubhouse. A membership committee, and so on. There is a reason for this system. All members in responsible positions are volunteers. They give freely of their time and expertise. They do this because they love their club and want the best for it. They work closely with the manager, and they expect the manager to carry out their policies smoothly and with maximum positive results.

In any club, there are forces at work twenty-four hours a day, seven days a week. Politics runs the show. Even in the best-run clubs in America, there is always something either visible or lurking beneath the surface that can bubble up on short notice.

When this happens, the fallout is usually unpleasant and frequently ugly.

This is the story of a modern-day golf and country club. Although it did not happen, it could have.

Robert B. Pile
Fall, 1998

The Players

Charles Ashley: The president of Pheasant Ridge, deeply involved in the highly volatile issue that shakes the Club.

Larry Costello: Secretary of the Club, an attorney, widely respected in the city and by his peers.

Claude Branch: General Manager of Pheasant Ridge. One of the new breed of club managers, college-trained. His position as manager is under fire, although his performance is at a acceptable level.

Chester Phillips: Long-time member of the Club, has served the Club in many capacities. Known for obsessive behavior and desire to control.

Frank Parsons: Long-time member of the Club, newly elected to the Board of Governors. A marketing consultant who becomes a key participant in an explosive incident in Club politics.

Lillian Thompson: Secretary to Club Manager Claude Branch. Handles many details of Club activities. Warm personality, well-liked by everyone. Unknowingly she becomes a part of the problem that may tear the Club apart.

Marianne Esterbrook: Comptroller of the Club. She is in charge of all matters pertaining to the billing of dues and charges to Club members. A chronic whiner, much disliked by the office staff.

Richard Kassel: A young attorney from one of the city's leading law firms. Hired by Pheasant Ridge to represent the Club in a defense of the charges by Chester Phillips.

Fred Webber: Attorney for Chester Phillips. He removes himself from his representation of Phillips as the problem increases.

Robert Newhouse: A very young attorney hired by Phillips to replace Webber.

Chapter One

The Annual Election

He pulled his car into the Club parking lot and steered into the last space available at the end of the row. He got out, started to walk away, then went back and locked the car doors. It's a helluva thing, he said to himself, when you've got to do this in the parking lot of your own golf club.

He walked up the hill to the clubhouse past the pro shop, where he waved to the Club professional still working in late afternoon. The pro saw him, walked out of the small area filled with clubs and merchandise, and extended his hand.

"Good luck tonight, Mr. Parsons. I hope you make it."

Parsons thanked him and walked into the main building. Pheasant Ridge Country Club was an earthy, traditional structure built in 1914, today still looking like an English manor house. The huge old clock over the door stood at 5:25. Frank had not realized it was that late, and he quickly walked upstairs to where the polls were about to close. He dropped his ballot into the box held by the Club secretary, who smiled at him.

"Good luck, Mr. Parsons. I was beginning to think you weren't going to make it on time."

He moved into the main lounge where several men were standing, laughing, and making small talk. Most of the men held coffee cups in their hands. The Club had a strict rule preventing the sale of liquor before and during its annual election of board members.

At the front of the room, which overlooked the golf course— still with snow on its fairways and greens—was a table with plates of appetizers, cheese, fruit, and crackers. Frank filled his plate and turned to join any friends he could spot. He was startled to note how few members he really knew. *My God*, he thought, *after thirty years, I'm a stranger in my own Club.*

At 5:40, the Club secretary came into the lounge area, and speaking as loudly as she could, said, "Gentlemen, the polls are now closed."

The members slowly filed in and sat down, leaving, as always, the first two rows in front vacant. Frank, seeing no empty chairs in other rows, sat at the end of the first row by himself. Because it was early spring, the golf course was not yet open to play and many members were still in the southern U.S., in Florida, Arizona, or California. The Club's annual meeting had for years been held in mid-March, in the days before few of the members went off to the South for the winter. Now, with many members retired and financially well-off, the mid-March meeting was probably too early in the year for strong attendance. The annual meeting was always on a Monday and in earlier days had always had near 100 percent participation.

1

The President of Pheasant Ridge, a relatively young man, walked to the lectern placed at the far end of the room. He tapped the microphone and said, "Is this damn thing working?"

Told that it was, he smiled and gestured at another young man sitting at the other end of the front row from Frank Parsons. To this man, he directed the question "Mr. Secretary, do we have a quorum?"

"Yes, Mr. President."

"Thank you. I now declare this an official meeting of the annual membership of this Club."

He looked down at his notes...then at the half-filled room. Several of these men had attended every annual meeting for many years. Some on the other hand were there for the first time. It was a kind of ritual, the annual meeting, with seldom anything said that was meaningful. For the Club president, it was a meeting to start and end as quickly as possible. The President, and all officers and board members present hoped that no one would raise a sticky issue, something to disturb the meeting.

For any country club in America, there are always issues that are controversial. In such cases, feelings on either side are usually emotional and often unpleasant. Such issues might range from something as simple as tee times on Sunday afternoons to major reconstruction of the clubhouse. There will always be a small group of members who systematically oppose anything recommended by the board of governors. Further, there is often a member, sometimes the same one year after year, who comes to the meeting for the single purpose of standing up and taking out his displeasure with the way the Club is being run. Such a man—and every club has at least one—is almost always talking without having any facts and is incapable of speaking clearly. No matter what point the member is trying to make, some members of the group will applaud. Most of the members, on the other hand, care little about what the man is saying and are anxious for the session to end so the bar will open.

In every annual meeting, members of the current board of governors usually sit together, banding together in a visual show of support for their president. One or two of them know that sometime during the meeting they may be asked by the president to stand and explain a given point. They, therefore, come armed with folders filled with relevant material to help clarify any issues.

The Club president, Charles Ashley, had had, by the standards of most club years, a relatively calm term in office. Still, he was happy that presiding over the meeting tonight would be his last official act as president. His feelings mixed. He was sad because he truly loved the Club and had enjoyed serving. But he also had a strong sense of relief that he was getting through his term without major problems or unpleasantness. After this meeting, the new board of governors, including ones elected tonight, would choose a new set of officers.

Ashley knew of no problem that might arise. But he had been around the inner workings of the Club for more than ten years and knew one could never be sure there wasn't something that could arise to spoil his final night. He was also aware that one particular member was always prepared, under certain circumstances, to take the floor. Ashley had one simple objective—get the meeting started and concluded.

He began to speak: "Ladies and gentlemen, I have had the privilege of serving as your president the past twelve months. I have really enjoyed it, believe me. Yes, there have been problems, but we have solved most of them. We have a magnificent golf course, still one rated among the top ten in the country. We have a full membership, which many clubs in the country today cannot say. We have a waiting list, a rarity in today's economy. We are in a good cash position, we have paid off our mortgage, and we are in pretty darned good shape.

"It is not my intent tonight to make a big speech. I'd like to keep this meeting moving right along. Only a few short committee reports will be made. There will be a short presentation made by our Grounds Committee chairman on some improvements that will be made on the golf course toward the end of the season when play is reduced. I think you will all be interested in that.

"Now, I'd like our Financial Committee chair, Fred LaTroy, to come up and tell you how we stand financially. Fred?"

At this point, the Club's financial head, a CPA with long experience in the Club's money matters, walked to the lectern. He was deeply respected by most of the membership, and Ashley did not anticipate problems.

LaTroy stood behind the lectern. "Is this damn thing working?" he said.

Chapter Two

The Trouble Begins

Four weeks before the annual meeting, Chester Phillips sat in his office and went over the list of candidates for the Pheasant Ridge Board of Governors. He took a yellow legal pad from his desk drawer and made a list of the names down the left-hand margin. He allowed considerable space between each name so he could make notes. He was a meticulous man, and he carefully lettered each name, very conscious of how the name looked on the page. No one would ever see the list, but it was important to him that it was neat and organized and had a professional look.

As he lettered, thoughts came to him about each man. He noted under one name "Lousy player," under another "Don't like his looks," under still another "Talked loud in the grill." In the space of an hour, he had accumulated under each name a significant number of comments. Very few were complimentary. Chester Phillips did not like very many people.

When he was finished, at least temporarily, he sat back, thinking about each man and whether a given individual would make a good board member for the Club. The longer he thought, the more it became clear to him that this list did not include more than one or two men he had any use for.

"It's a shitty group," he said out loud.

Under the name Frank Parsons he had written "Pretty old, only fair golfer. Member for long time. Probably his own man, probably can't be influenced. Not sure I like him, not sure how he feels about me. Better than most on the list. Might favor clubhouse remodeling!"

Chester Phillips had been a member of Pheasant Ridge for thirty-five years, first coming to the city as a salesman for his wife's heavy equipment firm. A good high school and college athlete, he immediately started looking for a golf club he could join. He was a seven-handicap player, and his job with his wife's company would allow him plenty of time to play. Golf was a good way to entertain customers, and there was no better way to do this than invite them to play at a first class club.

He made a list of every golf club in the area and quickly decided that of the several possibilities, only two were acceptable. One of the two was many miles from his home, much too far to drive several times a week. The second club, Pheasant Ridge, had a national reputation as one of the country's best golf courses. He decided that was the place for him.

That decision made, he moved quickly. He called a local stockbroker who had made some investments for him. He knew the man was a Pheasant Ridge member. He got right to the point.

"Carl, Chet Phillips. You're a member of Pheasant Ridge. I want to get in, and I want to move fast. What do I do?"

Once the process began, it moved quickly. Although Pheasant Ridge then as today had a membership waiting list, the stockbroker arranged to get an application. He hand-carried it to Phillips's office, showed him how to fill it out, then dropped it off at the Club office on his way home that evening. The stockbroker knew that his special effort would pay off. Chet Phillips, already a good customer, would advance quickly in his company and would soon be a major player in the market.

At that time, a Pheasant Ridge membership cost $1,500, a very modest amount by today's standards, but in 1960, this was not an amount the average young businessman had available to him. It was not a problem for Chet Phillips. The membership procedure called for adding a prospective member to the waiting list, after formal board of governors' approval. As membership openings became available, usually in the fall, the top name on the list would be called to see if he was ready to accept. If he was, he would pay the $1,500, and within a matter of days become a member. If the timing was right, he could still play several rounds of fall golf before the weather made it impossible. If, on the other hand, the prospective member was not ready to accept, his name went to the bottom of the list and all the others moved up a notch. It was a simple and workable system and it had been in place for many years.

In those days golf club memberships were routinely paid for by the man's employer if he was a valuable asset to the company. So if the applicant's entry costs were to be paid by his employer, the invitation to join was usually accepted on the spot. The money, called a "transfer fee," is used by most clubs for operating expenses to run the club on a day-to-day basis. This practice, however, slowly changed over the years, and transfer fees today have become part of a general fund used for capital improvements. In an old, long-established golf club with a clubhouse built many years ago, capital improvements become a necessity every few years to keep the building attractive and in operating efficiency. Pheasant Ridge was such a club, its clubhouse having been designed and built in the early 1920s.

Within one year of his arrival in the city, Chet Phillips became a member of Pheasant Ridge, sponsored by his stockbroker friend. Phillips's company gladly paid the $1,500 fee, recognizing that the small investment would be returned many times over. He immediately became a very active member, playing golf in the still-pleasant autumn weather at least twice a week and eating lunch with customers in the grill room frequently. Seldom did he bring his wife to the clubhouse, a circumstance noteworthy only because it was her family's money that was paying the bills. In his first year of membership, his wife entered the clubhouse only once.

Phillips, a promising salesman and a steady producer, did not use the Club merely for social purposes. He worked his membership, and over a period of time virtually all of his customers and potential customers enjoyed the privilege of playing this outstanding golf course. His handicap began at ten, and steadily went down, settling in at six.

Although he used the Club often, his use was mostly for business reasons. He was not an active participant in post-game conversation that is a key part of the enjoyment of golf. He did not drink and looked with open contempt on those who did.

He became active on two club committees, and by the end of his fourth year of membership had been elected to the board of governors. He then became chairman of the Club's most powerful group, the House Committee. A sound and instinctive businessman, he instituted several new practices to put the Club on a solid business basis. He was a ruthless cost cutter, willing to release a longtime employee on short notice if he felt the person was not performing. When he learned the assistant manager had been seen associating with a person suspected of being a homosexual, he had the man terminated.

"We're not going to have any queers in this Club," he told the members of the board.

When he had completed his list and made written comments about each prospective board member, Phillips took the Club roster from his desk. He then meticulously went through the entire book, first noting phone numbers of members he knew. He then selected names and phone numbers of members he knew but slightly. The two lists totaled nearly 200 of the Club's 300 golfing members. Because only golfing members were shareholders and therefore allowed to vote in the election, he ignored all other names in the roster such as Social, Tennis, and Intermediate members.

By the time he finished his list and check of the roster, it was three in the afternoon. He now settled himself in his chair and began to call each of the names on the first list. Before the afternoon was over, he would call about 75 of the total. At home in the evening, he would call another 50 or so.

His call to each member went the same: "This is Chet Phillips. The annual Club election is coming up and I know you agree with me we get the best guys on the board. I know you agree with me on the way our Club oughta be run and managed. I've got a list of guys here I think you should vote for."

He then read off his list recommending five of the ten running. In most cases, the members he called had received such a phone solicitation from Phillips every year. These men would normally respond to the call by saying "Okay," knowing that Phillips's interest was intense. Further, they had no desire to get into an argument with him. Occasionally, however, a member would respond thus: "Chet, I don't agree that Barney Olson is a good candidate. He's loud, and I don't entirely trust him."

In such cases Phillips would answer, "Well, you're wrong. He'd be good for the Club, and you'll be making a mistake by not voting for him."

He would then take his pencil and run it through the man's name on his list, which meant that the following year he would not call this fellow at all. Furthermore, he would not speak to the man again. Ever.

Once in a while, a member would respond with some heat. "Chet, I don't think we agree at all about the way the Club should be run. As a matter of fact, I don't like it that you call me each year and tell me how I should vote. I'll make up my own mind."

Phillips always answered the same way.

"Fuck you, then," and would hang up.

By the day of the meeting, Phillips had called 175 of the 200 men on his list. Not every call had produced the results he was after, but he was satisfied he could count on something like 130 votes for the slate he was recommending.

He had gone through this exercise every year since his fourth year as a Pheasant Ridge member. Each time it became more and more important to him to have impact on the board election. As the years passed, he became more obsessive, literally wanting to control the election process. Not only was the election itself important to him, but he felt failure if he did not get at least four of the five men he had recommended elected. As he continued to rise in the family business from salesman to sales manager to director of marketing and now to executive vice president, what was most important to him was his ever-increasing influence over everything that went on at Pheasant Ridge.

One of his strategies for domination of virtually every phase of Club activity was his determination to set the annual election earlier in the spring. There was nothing specific about this in the Club's bylaws, simply that there must be an election each year. In the early days of the Club and for many years after, the exodus of many members to the southern U.S. during the winter months was not a meaningful occurrence. Now, however, with perhaps a good one-third of the members literally gone from October through April, this migration was a significant factor in Club operation.

An early date for the annual election would mean that Phillips could more realistically manipulate the election results. Over a period of time, he had convinced many Club members that the early election was in the Club's best interests.

"What the hell," he said, "those bastards don't give a damn about this place. It's us who stay here who really count."

It was a convincing argument. It went like this: Those who went south for the winter were the very old members, often called "old farts." These men contributed nothing to the Club, playing golf slowly and cluttering up the course.

"I'm in favor of slowly weeding these guys out," he said to anyone who would listen. "It'll make this place better for those of us who really help the Club and who like to play in four hours or less."

In spreading this line of thinking, it had never occurred to Chet Phillips that one day he too would be in the age category he so despised. At age fifty-seven, he was still in excellent health, at the top of his golf game, and would be the next chief executive officer of his company. When the day came that he would have to slow down (a realism that was never part of his thinking) his capacity for rationalizing any point of view that he held would allow for an adjustment favorable to him.

His strategy had proved to be astonishingly successful. Most members care little about the way their Club is run, wanting only the best possible golf course, decent food and service, and a nice building to enjoy an evening out. They are unconcerned about the politics of running the Club or its power structure, both of which were a literal obsession with Chester Phillips.

This year, with the annual meeting earlier than ever, due to his relentless efforts, a good 35 percent of the membership was not present. Like any good politician, Chet Phillips could count.

Following the report by the Club's finance committee head, President Ashley, introduced two more committee chairs. Each man delivered a short report and quickly sat down, relieved to have a potential ordeal over and done.

Ashley said "Within a few minutes, we'll have the results of the count for the election to the board. I'll announce the names, and then we're done and can go to dinner."

Chet Phillips stood up. Chuck Ashley groaned inwardly, knowing that whatever Phillips might have to say, it would be controversial and unpleasant. There was a murmur in the room, most members having been through this many times. "Here we go again," some of them said aloud.

Chet Phillips, a smirk on his face, said, "Mr. President, I have an issue I believe is very important."

Chapter Three

The Motion

Ashley, outwardly calm, said "Yes, Mr. Phillips, you may use one of the microphones placed around the room for this purpose."

"I'd like to use the mike you're using, Mr. President, that one, that one at the head of the room." Again the mirthless smile dared Ashley to deny him use of the mike that would allow him to dominate the room.

"Mr. Phillips, you may use any mike you wish," said Ashley, not smiling.

"Thank you, Mr. President, it's an honor to be able to use the same mike as the president of the Club."

He walked to the lectern, took the mike from its holder, and walked around to the front, now holding the mike in his hand. He played the moment for all it was worth, the smile still on his face totally absent of humor.

"Mr. President, and members, I have what I think is a timely subject to discuss. It has to do with the officers of this Club, that is, those four men who will be elected by the new board to the four positions, the men who basically run the Club. This group automatically becomes the executive committee: president, vice president, treasurer, and secretary. As I say, traditionally this group is elected by the new board of governors. In effect, what takes place is that five men who have never served on the board will be casting votes for who will sit on the new executive committee. These new men have no idea whether the board members they might vote for are competent to run this Club for the next twelve months. Or even the next twelve minutes."

Phillips paused, the smirk was still on his face. He listened with pleasure to the murmurs now being heard, knowing he had full attention of the membership.

"Mr. President, I believe it is against the best interests of this Club to have such a critically important group elected partly by brand new members of the board. Members who are still wet behind the ears when it comes to Club policies and operations. Because the executive committee is so important, the decisions they make so impactful, I propose we change the procedure by which they are elected. Our procedure, I might add, is a rubber stamp. I have studied the bylaws on this issue and there is nothing that says we cannot institute a new way of doing it. The bylaws merely state that when the new board convenes, a slate of officers will be elected, and that group will be the new executive committee. I propose that we select a specific number of Club members from the attendance, and that they join the new members of the board and participate in the election of

9

officers. I would propose that there be five such men and their sole duty would be their temporary participation in the first meeting of the new board, with the authority to cast their votes for a new slate of officers. My reasoning for this proposal is to offset, through the votes of this additional group, a possible mistake by the new board members in helping to elect one or more officers not competent for the job."

There was an immediate stirring in the room, as some members slowly began to understand what Phillips was trying to do.

Phillips continued, his smile now a mocking grin. "Mr. President, I realize this is a totally new idea. But I have thought a lot about it, and I think it makes sense. It's fair, and it will help ensure that our executive committee is representative of the total membership, not just the board. To make this proposal official, I make a motion to that effect, and I demand, as is my right, that the motion is voted on at this meeting. Right now."

He turned to Ashley. "Let's see you walk away from that one," he said in a stage whisper.

There was scattered applause from the membership.

Chuck Ashley was stunned. Of all the possible problems that could have come up, this one was totally unexpected. He was not a strict parliamentarian, and he had executed the duties of the president's office the past year mostly based on courtesy, common sense, and instinct. He had been, in fact, a marvelous chief executive.

As a businessman running his own company, he was used to making quick decisions, but now he had no ready response. His instinct told him there was something wrong with the idea, but if, as Phillips had said, there was nothing in the bylaws to prevent the idea from becoming policy, he was not sure how to proceed. Knowing Phillips, he knew the proposal was purely self-serving.

He began to speak. "This is a tough one. Frankly, I'm not sure how to address it. Obviously, there must be discussion. And I will remind us all that there is a motion on the floor. I do have a question, however, before we go any further. Mr. Phillips, do you have the men in mind you would wish to act as this special group?"

Phillips nodded. "Yes, I have all five names right here in my hand."

"I thought so," said Chuck Ashley and there was laughter.

He continued. "Larry Costello, you're our legal expert and you're the present secretary of the Club. Do you have a comment?"

Costello stood and walked to the microphone. He was unsmiling, and though he did not look at Phillips, his face showed the contempt he felt.

"Mr. President, I have no quick glib answer to this proposal. Anything I say at this point is strictly off the top of my head. So I'll deal with it in that light."

He then looked directly at Chet Phillips, who was basking in the situation he had brought about.

Costello continued. "I feel the idea is out of order. It may be true our bylaws do not deal directly with this issue. Mr. Phillips may be correct on that point. However, if they don't, I'm sure there is a reason why not. But without studying them further on this specific point, I think we could be making a serious, serious mistake to take a vote, regardless of the motion on the floor. Mr. Phillips may have the right to make the motion, but I am asking him now to withdraw it until we have studied the matter thoroughly and can get back to the membership. Mr. President, I ask that you request Mr. Phillips to withdraw his motion. As a matter of procedure, I don't recall that there was a second to the motion?"

Ashley looked around the room. There was no second. The room was silent.

Ashley, hugely relieved, then turned to Costello. "Mr. Secretary, there being no second, is it correct that the motion need not be acted upon?"

Costello nodded.

There was now mild applause, which soon became heavy and came from most of the assembled members, who for the most part recognized that it was not wise to pursue such an idea without the study obviously called for.

Chet Phillips, his face red, stood up. "Mr. President, I can see that most members present now appear to be against me. I do not, Mr. Secretary, agree with you. If you want to study it, that is your job, I guess. But I've already studied it, and I had my lawyer study it. I think you lack the guts to face the issue. But I'd like your official response in writing, and I'd like the membership informed in writing—no later than one week from today. That's not a request. That's a demand!"

Costello did not stand up. He looked directly at Ashley.

"Mr. President, the request—the demand—is totally out of order. I cannot and will not address it that quickly, nor will I be bullied. I have a law practice and the demands on my time are particularly heavy right now. But even if they weren't, I would not accede to such a demand!"

Phillips stood up. His face was now twisted in a snarl. "I'll sue your ass!" he said to Larry Costello.

Ashley, shaken and angry but also relieved, returned to the microphone.

"I had hoped this meeting, which is the end of my term of office, would be calm and peaceful." He smiled ruefully. "Obviously, I was wrong. I have only this to add. This Club has almost always been run by honorable, hard-working men. That has certainly been true of the current group on the board. Your board will not be shoved around, I promise you that. We will deal fairly with issues raised and usually, I think, we end up doing what is right.

"Now, while all this has been going on, I have been handed a piece of paper with the names of the new board members. I'll announce their names and ask you to hold your applause until all have been introduced." (No one, of course, would pay any attention to this suggestion. Applause would follow each name).

"William Farmer, Newton Carlson, Casey Tolles, Frank Parsons, Sherman Floyd. Gentlemen, take a bow."

Ashley now took a deep breath. "Gentlemen, I will entertain a motion for adjournment."

The motion was made and seconded and the members left the room in small groups. The name of Chet Phillips was on the lips of many of them.

Along with Chuck Ashley, the board now convened in the Club's formal dining room. Although the purpose of the meeting was to elect the slate of officers, Larry Costello got Ashley to one side and made a quiet suggestion. Ashley listened, then nodded.

As the group took their seats around the table, Costello stood up.

"Gentlemen, in light of what just happened in there, I have a suggestion. I have run this by President Ashley, and he reluctantly agrees." He looked at Ashley and smiled.

"What I'm going to say now is off the record, and since I'm the Club secretary, I guess I can promise you these remarks will not appear in the minutes. To you newly elected members, I will only say that `off the record' means the matter should not be discussed outside this meeting. I know Chet Phillips very well, as some of you do. You know, as I do, he is a strange combination of a pretty smart guy and a thoroughly screwed-up human being. He is vindictive, vengeful, and never forgets. He will never forget that for the moment, I beat him in there, and he will never rest until he has some kind of revenge.

"But the hell with that! I'm far more concerned about his motion. He did not make the recommendation lightly. Obviously he is trying as he usually does to control damn near everything that happens in this Club. If we had hastily approved that motion and let it become Club policy, no one knows what might happen. But for now, at the very least it would have meant that he could have pretty well controlled who became the new officers of this board. For you guys who are perhaps friends of Chet's, I am urging you not to repeat these remarks to him. As I have said, they are `off the record' but I also want you to know that I will be bloody upset if any of this comes back to me. Now here is what I am proposing and will make a motion on. You can be sure that Phillips will follow up in some way; he'll try like hell to keep this issue alive, and so we've got to be smart. I propose we do not elect any new officers, that we do nothing, that we allow the current officers to remain in their positions for the near and per-haps longer-term future. This not only will allow us time to really study the matter and discuss it here, but it will cut across his idea. He will not like it, and he'll see what we've tried to do, but there's nothing he can do about it. We are not required to elect new officers, we always have the option of allowing the present officers to stay in office. And I now make a motion to that effect. And yes, I got Ashley's permission—as I told you— that he would remain in office for the unspecified future. Sorry, Chuck, I know you were counting on retirement."

Ashley called for a second to the motion and asked for a vote, which was unanimous in support. And the new members saw that in Larry Costello they had a shrewd man thinking in the best interests of the Club.

Chuck Ashley looked around the room. "I welcome you new board members. I pray that what we witnessed tonight is now behind us, and I know that for the coming three years, we'll go forward together without any more unpleasantness."

Ashley knew that was far too optimistic. But he had no idea what was ahead. Had he known, he probably would have resigned on the spot.

Chapter Four

Frank Parsons

The Pheasant Ridge Board of Governors was made up of sixteen male shareholders. Each golfing member of the Club owned a share of stock in the Club. This he received when he paid his entry fee, called "transfer." The term of a board member lasted three years, and any member whose term was ending with the annual meeting was usually given the courtesy of running for a second term. To such an offer, about half the board members would accept, the others decline. The main reason for declining was that the board member simply did not have the time to devote beyond the three years. Most of these who declined had also become so fed up with Club politics that at the end of three years, they had had enough.

Board membership in any golf club is an honor, but at Pheasant Ridge, like most clubs, the time in office could be very painful, with personal abuse from non-board members a particularly loathsome part of the package. This personal abuse and petty politics are key reasons why many highly competent men refuse to run. They know that abuse and criticism go with their jobs in business, but they rationalize that at least they get paid for it. Serving on a golf club board they are strictly volunteers, and they know going in that the hours will be long and the problems often frustrating at the very least, and almost as often pure horror.

As a new board member, Frank Parsons had a pretty good idea what he was letting himself in for. But he felt he could make a contribution. He loved the club, he loved the game of golf, and he looked forward to the next three years.

No one could have foreseen what was about to happen. The next twelve to twenty-four months would prove to be the most traumatic period in the history of one of Americas most prestigious golf and country clubs.

Parsons was retired and had spent most of his business life as a marketing consultant. He had worked first for a large consumer products company where he rose to executive vice president. He then left to form his own consulting firm and had done well. In his late fifties and in good health, he turned the business over to his oldest son and called it quits. However, he continued to serve a few medium and small companies and found his services were in considerable demand. So he worked at this half days and when the golf season started, he would devote the largest part of most days to playing the game. What Parsons wanted more than anything was to get his handicap under ten. He would never achieve that goal.

His wife had died years ago. He had three children. The two boys had finished college and were holding good jobs. His daughter passed the opportunity to go on to school to get married.

During his thirty-seven years in business, he had lived with corporate politics, game-playing, and tyranny. He felt he had seen just about every form of personal petty behavior and meanness, but even his tough skin would be put to the test in the coming months of his board service.

He had once worked with a client advertising manager who kept a daily record of mistakes and personal slights on the part of his coworkers. Eventually this manager used this record to get his own boss fired. He also used the meticulous notes as leverage against the ad agency people with whom he worked. On an annual basis he would ask the president of the agency to come over to his office and would go over in detail the weaknesses and failings of each agency person who worked on his account. He even kept records of the indecision and mistakes in judgement made by his own chief executive officer. At any given time, the man could have made a solid case against virtually anyone with whom he worked.

At one time, Frank Parsons had been victimized by this man. He seldom thought about it any more. But after exposure to Chet Phillips, he saw that the ad manager had been a minor league player. Parsons knew that Phillips would continue to stir the pot, would make moves to get revenge. Parsons saw Chuck Ashley was one Phillips target, and another, of course, would be Larry Costello. At this time he did not foresee that he himself would soon be in the line of fire.

Frank made a practice of working in the office in his home every morning for at least four hours. He could easily fill these hours. He wrote marketing plans for this client, gave some advice on product pricing to another client, helped one CEO write his annual report. He loved the work and was good at it. The fees he received were substantial and the income, on top of his retirement plan, allowed him to live a very good life. When he had made the decision to run for the Pheasant Ridge Board, he knew the job would be time-consuming. So he told two of his clients he would have to cut back on his service to them.

At this point he wanted to do something positive for the Club. And he told Ashley, whom he liked very much, that he was ready to take on a job, any job, anything the Club needed.

Chapter Five

The House Committee

On Tuesday afternoon following the board meeting, Chuck Ashley called Parsons and asked him to make a lunch meeting downtown, not at the Club.

Ashley got right to the point. "Frank, I'd like to have you take on the job of chairing the House Committee. I won't kid you. It's the toughest job in the joint, as tough as being president. Well, maybe not that tough."

He grinned. Ashley was a positive man. He did not carry grudges and anything bad that had happened yesterday was forgotten in the new day. He was a tireless worker. At age forty- five, he ran his family's company and did it very well. He had an easy manner, a warm smile, and was, Parsons had determined earlier, a man who could be completely trusted.

He looked at Parsons now. I hope you'll say `yes.' You may hate me a year from now, but I know you'll do a great job. You're by far the best man on the board for House."

Frank had no trouble answering. "If that's what you want me to do, Chuck, you got it."

"Wonderful!" Ashley was obviously relieved and pleased. "Okay, get a committee together, anyone you want. It's your call. Now you may or may not know that House covers everything connected to the physical plant. Everything except the Pro Shop. That's Corey's responsibility. House also includes food and drink. You'll be working with the head chef and the restaurant managers. They're all good people. And your closest man on the staff will be Claude Branch. I've worked with him, of course. Frankly, I don't know how good he is. But he's a nice young man and he means well. He doesn't want to offend anyone, and maybe that's his worst problem. He's pretty good with the financial end, and he's a good computer guy. But he'll do anything you want, and you can depend on him if he tells you something.

"He's got some enemies, as any club manager does. You're bound to offend someone. It's usually a wife, they're the worst. And you can bet that one of his enemies is Chet Phillips." He grimaced as he said the name.

"Anyway, the job's yours, and you'll get 100 percent support from me. Keep me informed. And keep the board informed. I know you'll do that. Hell, you've been in the big time. You certainly know more than I do about handling yourself. Good luck, my friend."

x x x x x x

According to the National Golf Foundation, there are approximately 4,500 private golf clubs in the U.S. Precise figures are hard to come by, because there is no central authority or clearinghouse that can state a figure absolutely. Further, there is some blurring between what is a private club, a semi-private club, and a purely public club. Each year new clubs are formed and other clubs change status. Several clubs go under each year for purely financial reasons. There are many relatively new clubs built as the center of a golf environment, and memberships come automatically with the purchase of a home on the course. Several courses done by Jack Nicklaus for instance, operate this way.

Golf in America today is a very dynamic reality. The number of golfers increases each year. The amount of money spent on golf equipment and apparel is huge. A home on a fine golf course designed by a big name such as Nicklaus can go for $1 million or much more. A plot of ground on a course can sell for a half million. In such a layout, the golf course and clubhouse become the center of the members' lives. Families eat regularly at the Club, and both husbands and wives may play golf several times a week. Clubs of this kind are springing up everywhere in the country, often on ground that for years has been barren desert, or marsh or the forgotten foothills of mountains.

On the other hand, there is the traditional golf club built in the twenties. The founders, bound by a love of the game, put up the original money and found a location usually at the edge of their city, possibly on farm land. They hired well-known golf architects, famous names, often men born in Scotland who, for a relatively small amount of money, would travel to the location and design a wonderful layout that would still be a real test 50, 75, and 100 years later. Clubhouses built in those times were traditional in style and conformed to basic needs of members. There would be a formal dining area, men's lounge, men's locker room, and a small pro shop. The founders would search for a professional to hire, and when on board, he would run the pro shop and provide lessons for the members. If the club grew and prospered (not all of them did) the clubhouse would gradually be expanded, the golf course would need periodic upgrading (such as a watering system), and the pro would hire an assistant. The assistant would be paid a small wage and could make extra money giving lessons.

Most of the big-time clubs in America today are professionally managed. A full-time, specially trained man runs the club's day-to-day business. The job is increasingly sophisticated. A well-known prestigious club may have as many as 500 golfing members, another 800 non-golfers called "social members," as well as members who play only tennis. Dues paid by these various categories vary, with golfers paying the largest monthly rates. A golf club today in America is no longer merely a place for men. Increasingly, it has become a family haven, and facilities for non-golfers, women, and children have been required. Most clubs have swimming pools, tennis courts, even exercise and weight rooms. There are still formal dining rooms, but personal habits have changed, and an informal grill area has become far busier. Restaurant management skills are a must, members demand good food and reasonable prices. Service is critically important. Wait staffs must be trained by people who know the business. Food must be intelligently purchased and waste controlled in every way.

All of the big clubs have well-paid managers, and many have assistant managers because the work load is heavy and the demands far beyond a nine-to-five routine. Even modestly-sized clubs have found they need a good manager to install operating disciplines. Most managers today have had special college training, and courses in club management are common at many colleges and universities.

As the job of club managers has become more specialized, so too has the role of the club professional. No longer is the pro a captive in his pro shop, not particularly welcome in the clubhouse and only on the golf course in unusual circumstances. Today, the club pro is also a specialist with training in finance, inventory control, and marketing. Most clubs pay their pro a modest salary, and he can make significant income not just through lessons but also running a fine retail store with the latest merchandise and shrewd pricing. Today's pro is a college graduate who can and does mix frequently with members and may play golf as many as two or three times a week. He is very likely a person of considerable charm who can hold his own conversationally with any member.

Further, the increase in women players has resulted in clubs hiring a female professional available for lessons to the membership. It is not at all unusual to find in the pro shop the head pro, two or three male assistants, and a female assistant. In a modern dynamic club, they all keep busy. The younger ones still work on their games in off hours, and all dream of a greater future in golf, either on the several pro tours, or as head of their own golf operation at another club. These assistants are virtually all college graduates and well-trained in club operations. In the ranks of assistant pros can be found some of the finest and brightest young men and women in our country.

The manager at a large, prestigious club may draw a salary of six figures, and he holds considerable power. In some clubs the manager may also carry the title of chief operating officer. As such he carries out the direction given him by the club's board and president. He has day to day responsibility for all areas of club operations with the exception of the pro shop. The club manager and the club pro are today of equal status. Both jobs are critically important, and clubs today demand and get very strong people who would probably be successful in many areas of business.

The club manager job can be difficult and highly stressful. At any given time, his relationships with various members of the club may be tenuous. On any given day, he might slight a member's wife or somehow offend a longtime member. His smile to one member may be friendly and sincere, to another devious and suspicious. He is expected to know the name of every member and call them by name when he sees them. He is expected to have a ready answer to any question. If there is something wrong, he must see that it is fixed immediately. So fragile is the job security that written contracts have now become common. The average tenure of a club manager in any case is slightly less than five years.

Claude Branch, the club manager at Pheasant Ridge, had held the job nearly three years. He had proved to be very good with employee personnel and had attracted two very key staff people as grill manager and executive chef. Under the direction of these two, the club's food operation was the best it had ever been. He was strong in finance, computer-trained, and his relationship with the club professional was positive.

On the negative side he was seen by some members as cold and impersonal and was still unable to identify more than a few members by their names. In an instance where his job hung in the balance, it was unlikely he would have the support of more than half the membership. The position of the board had not been tested. As Frank Parsons joined the board and became chair of the club's most important committee, the position of Claude Branch was hardly one of real strength.

Chapter Six

The Manager

On Monday afternoon following the board meeting, Branch called his secretary into his office. He told her to bring her file. The file was thick, and for the next two hours the two went over every item.

The secretary, Lillian Thompson, had strong people skills and was very loyal to the Club. She was also the official membership secretary, which meant she kept track of all the records of each member, a time-consuming responsibility. She had limited secretarial ability, could not take shorthand, and was a poor speller and careless typist. Branch was very aware of her mechanical shortcomings, but knew she was strong in the important work the Club needed, and thus kept her on. A more demanding manager would have insisted on better spelling and grammar. He had on three occasions commented on her spelling weakness and got an immediate flood of tears. He did not bring the subject up again.

When they finished with the file, he sat back and smiled at her. "Well, Lillian, we got a lot of work done, half of which I should have finished last week, but there's so much going on here, I haven't had time to do the job I'm paid to do."

"Claude," said the young woman, "I don't know how you keep up with things, I really don't. You seem to be able to keep lots of balls in the air."

"Lillian, it probably seems that way, but sometimes I don't feel I can really do the job needed here. Some of it is fun and even exciting, but some is pure agony."

She looked at him. She had never heard him doubt himself in any way. She changed the subject. "What do you think of the new board members? Are they going to be able to do the job?" It was a question she only asked to shift her boss away from a subject that seemed to trouble him.

"I don't really know much about any of them. Except maybe Frank Parsons. He's been around quite a while. He's a good Club member. Never causes trouble, a real gentleman. I've heard he was good at his job in advertising and marketing. I think he'll be very good for this place. I'll find out for sure as I work with him on House.

"A word to you about him. I have a feeling he can be very tough—not mean, but very tough. He'll be writing lots of reports and he'll expect them to be typed promptly and accurately. I know he runs a tight meeting. He has been in a very tough business and I doubt he could have gotten by with less than top performance. He'll expect a lot out of you. I'll do my best to run some interference for you, but mostly you'll be on your own." He stopped and looked at her for a sign of tears.

She smiled. "I know what you mean, Claude, and I'll try."

"I know you will. I don't mean to scare you, I'm just being realistic.

Incidentally, Lillian, you seem to be hurting a bit?"

"Yes, I'm in some pain in my neck. It's stiff. Too much sitting and not enough exercise."

"Stiff neck, huh? Turn your chair around and I'll give you a little neck massage. I do that for my wife, and she says I'm pretty good at it."

As Lillian turned her chair around so that her back was to Branch, he walked over to her, bringing his hands up to the back of her neck. He began to slowly rub his fingers over the area between her hair line and the collar of her dress.

At this point, one of the female office workers walked by Branch's open office door. Rather than continue on her errand, she walked back to her office. She got out a yellow pad, and wrote these words:

Monday afternoon. 3 P.M.—Branch massaging Thompson.

Chapter Seven

Phillips Makes a Move

Chet Phillips knew he had been bloodied at the annual meeting. Following the meeting, he spent the better part of two days in a rage, talking to himself as he drove his car. He brooded about it as he went to bed. At his office he found it hard to concentrate on his work. After the second day, he made a decision.

The morning of the third day, he got to his office earlier than usual, at 6:30 A.M. He scribbled a quick note to his secretary, who would not be in until 8, telling her he did not want to be disturbed. His office door would be closed. He then got out a yellow pad and went to work on his plan. After a half hour he had covered five pages, and in his tight, disciplined lettering, had made a list of ten items on the last page. The first item read "Get everything on Ashley," the second "Get all dope on each board member," the third "Dig into Costello." The list continued on through nine. Then he sat back to think about what he had done so far. He then added a tenth: "Find out about Parsons. Talk to his clients."

He continued to fill the pages until by a few minutes after 8:30 he felt he had taken the plan as far as it would go at this time. He checked his watch and knew by now the Club offices were open and staff people would be at work. He dialed the Club and asked for the comptroller, whom he knew slightly. Her name was Marianne Esterbrook, and she had worked for Pheasant Ridge for about five years. He had heard that she and Manager Claude Branch did not particularly like each other. He knew further that she apparently had few friends among the office personnel.

"Marianne, this is Mr. Chet Phillips. We know each other, right?"

The young woman, suddenly scared, said "Yes, sir, Mr. Phillips, I know who you are."

"Okay, Marianne, I am working on a confidential project for the Club. It is critically important, and I am going to need information. There are only two people who know about this, and I don't want you to talk to anyone about this. Is that understood?"

The girl, now increasingly nervous, was at the same time intrigued. Why would a member of Mr. Phillips stature want to talk with her about something so significant?

"Yes, Mr. Phillips, I understand. But I don't know what it is you want."

"Marianne, I would like to meet with you as soon as possible, this evening if you can manage it."

"Yes, sir. I've got to visit my mother at the hospital tonight. Before 6:00 P.M. Is that okay?"

"Yes, Marianne, that's fine. Wonderful! Let's see, you get off at 5, right? Do you know where Barton's Coffee Shop is? It's less than a half mile from the Club. Meet me at the coffee bar as soon as you can get there after 5. I'll be there waiting. Do you know what I look like? Will you recognize me?"

"Yes, sir, I know what you look like."

"Fine. See you a little after 5. Oh, and Marianne, you are doing the Club a great service. We appreciate it."

Marianne Esterbrook put down her phone. Her hands were shaking. She had no idea what Phillips wanted to see her about, but she was excited about a secret meeting with a member of the Club who obviously was a person of considerable clout. She knew that any project Phillips would be working on had to be very important. The more she thought about it, the more intrigued she became. Marianne Esterbrook was attracted to power.

She was also the person who had seen Claude Branch massaging the neck of his secretary.

At 5:05, Phillips parked his car in the small lot in front of Barton's Coffee Shop. At this time of day it was not crowded, although every morning the shop would have been filled and no parking space in front. He walked into the shop, ordered coffee, and waited.

He watched a few minutes later as Marianne Esterbrook got out of her car and walked to the shop's front door. He noticed that she was an attractive young woman, stylishly dressed.

She walked to where he was sitting and said, "Good evening, Mr. Phillips." She was again uncomfortable and wondered if she should have come. She waited for Phillips to speak.

"Marianne, I thank you for being willing to meet me. Let me quickly caution you not to use my name as you just did. There are good reasons for this. I don't want it known that we are meeting. As I've said, this is a very confidential project. You are in a position to be very helpful and of real value to the Club."

He paused and looked directly at her. He had chosen Esterbrook only after thinking about every employee who worked in the Club office. Not only did he know that she was the comptroller, but he had checked her out thoroughly. She was not popular with her fellow employees, and was intensely disliked by most of them. She was a whiner, a constant trouble-maker, a person who would talk to one employee to gain information, then turn and tell another employee that the first person could not be trusted. It gave her real pleasure to sow seeds of doubt about each employee in the minds of others. Her constant objective, day in, day out, was to gather information about her boss Claude Branch that would lead to his eventual dismissal from Pheasant Ridge.

She was perfect for what Phillips had in mind.

"Marianne, I'll get right to it. You, as comptroller of the Club, have access to information we really need to do a thorough job on this project. You have facts available to you having to do with the member's bills. You know their payment records. You know what's out of line. You know the phonies."

As he said the word "phonies," his voice became harsh and his face twisted in disgust. Again Marianne felt a twinge of fear. This was not a man she wanted as an enemy.

"Specifically, Marianne, I need to have the payment records of all the board members. I need to see their monthly bills, the chits they sign for lunch, for golf, for parties. For every occasion. I especially need, as soon as you can give it to me, the payment facts about Mr. Charles Ashley. It is

21

my understanding he has some special billing arrangement with the office. Is that correct?"

He paused to note her reaction. It was part of his plan that if at this point she would refuse his request, he had a fifty- dollar bill ready in his pocket. If she was willing to go along, the fifty would not change hands.

She was silent for a moment. "Gee, I don't know, Mr. Phillips. I could get in a lot of trouble. I'm not sure I should even be talking to you."

Phillips made an instant decision. "Marianne, this is so important that I am authorized to reward you for your willingness to help us."

He leaned heavily on the word "us" to give the young woman reason to think there were others involved in this secret project. He was correct in his feeling that this would make her feel more comfortable. He took the fifty from his pocket and folded it, then got it into her hand with the least possible movement. The second she took the money without looking at it, Phillips knew he had her.

"Marianne," he said soothingly, "It is critically important to this Club that you help us. You are the only person we can trust."

This was a master stroke.

"Well, all right, Mr. Phillips, if it will help the Club. I like the Club. I want the best for it. I can get what you need. It will take time, but I'll get it. You are right that Mr. Ashley has a special arrangement about his bill. I don't see anything wrong with it, but it is unusual. Because Mr. Ashley has several relatives who are members of the Club—a brother, and I believe, his father, and some cousins, I think—-we help simplify his bill paying."

Phillips smiled. Inwardly, he was delighted.

"Thank you, Marianne. I knew you wouldn't disappoint us. Now, as you check the bills of Mr. Ashley, be sure to make notes about anything you feel is out of line. Anything. Why do you think he handles his bills this way? This way you say is `unusual'?"

"I'm not sure, Mr. Phillips. I suppose because there are several Ashleys, it helps to keep things straight if we do what he has asked. All the Ashley bills are paid with one check each month."

"One check? You mean one check for the whole crowd of them?"

"Yes, sir. We've been doing that for some time."

"I see. Well, thank you, Marianne. I'll let you go now. Please get this stuff to me as soon as you possibly can. Obviously, Marianne, if there's something funny going on, we need to know about it. And we don't want Mr. Ashley to know that we know. Do you understand?"

"Yes, sir, I think I do. I'll do the best I can. Sir, I've got to leave now. My mother expects me the same time each day at the hospital."

"Fine, Marianne. You run along. We won't forget this service on your part."

Chapter Eight

Marianne Esterbrook

Phillips had done his background checking on Marianne Esterbrook, and by the time he first met her, he was fairly confident she was the right person to be his mole. Not only could she get him figures he wanted, but he also felt she was be a continuing source of information once he got to know her and she felt comfortable with him. Now that the two had met, he was completely satisfied he had found the right person to help him carry out his plan.

Esterbrook was an unhappy young woman, unhappy as a child, unhappy as an adult. Although she had a natural aptitude for figures and a good grasp of finance, she was so difficult to work with the people in her department despised her. She could not keep any kind of continuity in her small staff. The resulting turnover was very wasteful. The longest tenure of any person who worked for her was but eleven months. She was physically attractive, but her personality so poisonous that no one wanted to be around her. She was dissatisfied with her job, her pay, the small office given her, and she liked no one in the entire office of the Club.

She hated Claude Branch, not for any specific reason, merely that he was her boss. She hated Lillian Thompson even more. She thought Thompson was saying things behind her back, which, incidentally, was not true. Thompson was a straight arrow, and office intrigue was not her style. In fact, Thompson avoided Marianne as much as possible. Their jobs did not overlap. It was impossible, however, for Thompson not to hear some of Esterbrook's constant whining. On one occasion Lillian spoke up.

"Marianne, you are your own worst enemy. You complain all the time. If you worked as hard as you complain, you'd do a far better job and you'd be happier. I'm sorry, but that's the truth. And I don't appreciate your complaining about Mr. Branch. He is a fine man, and he's my boss. I won't stand for any more of your critical remarks about him."

Esterbrook, unable to take this blunt but well-meaning criticism, walked away, tossing her head. She quickly made up her mind to get even with the secretary. She would accomplish it somehow.

It was at this particular period of her life that Chet Phillips made his contact with her. Phillips was the kind of man who made it a point to find out what employees were like and how they felt about each other. It was yet another obsession. He had learned that she regularly hit Branch for pay increases. He also discovered she had frequently asked Branch for flexible hours because of her mother's prolonged illness. Branch had turned her down. He had also turned down her request for a larger office. Phillips knew he could use her hatred of Branch for his own purposes.

And because of the extremely sensitive nature of her job, Phillips knew she would be able to unearth every conceivable piece of information about any given member. Esterbrook would know, for instance, which members were consistently late in paying their bills. She would know which members regularly asked for adjustments in their monthly invoices for food and beverage. From her, he could find out about in-office romances, poor attendance records, and who got special favors from Branch, anything that would give him an edge in carrying out his plan.

Within two months after the annual meeting, Chet Phillips had decided he wanted the resignation of Manager Claude Branch. He also would ask for the resignation or removal from office of Charles Ashley, and the same from Larry Costello. His hit list also included the restaurant manager and the executive chef.

As the days went by and he did not hear from Esterbrook, he became increasingly impatient. In his own business, he was accustomed to instant reaction to his demands. He felt he had given Esterbrook ample time to dig up at least part of what he wanted.

On this particular afternoon, exactly one week after his meeting with her at the coffee shop, he picked up his phone and dialed her number.

"Marianne, this is your friend. Don't say my name. What have you got for me?"

"I'm almost through with it, sir." She could not resist telling him she had worked nights to dig up the information. "I can put it in the mail this afternoon. Most of it is done. There are only a couple of minor things I have not had time to check. I have been very busy up here. Mr. Branch has asked for a study of supplier costs and I've had to work late doing that too."

"That's wonderful, I mean not that you've had to work late, but that you got my stuff. It's coming to my office, right?"

"Yes, sir, I understood that's where you wanted it."

"Right. I'll expect it tomorrow. Oh, and Marianne, one more thing. Is there some other Club employee who feels the way you do, who feels the Club is being poorly run? Who feels lots of employees are getting away with things? Can you give me a name?"

"Yes, sir, there's a salad chef who talks to me from time to time. She tells me of lots of problems in the kitchen. People are stealing things, coming in late, leaving early, stuff like that."

"Can you give me her name?"

"Yes, it's Gert. Gertrude Carlson. She's been here for years."

"Gertrude Carlson. I'm writing it down. Thank you. Marianne, I'll look forward to getting the information you've gathered."

Phillips smiled to himself. "Getting somewhere," he muttered.

Marianne Esterbrook, sitting in her chair in her tiny office, looked out the window and her thought was *Now I'll show these people around here.*

Phillips clapped his hands in satisfaction. Marianne Esterbrook decided she'd take herself to lunch today rather than eat in the employee lounge.

Chapter Nine

The Brown Envelope

The lunch meeting between Ashley and Parsons had been delayed several times because of busy work schedules. When they finally met, late spring had arrived and the golf season had begun. It was a time of year when lovers of golf think frequently about hitting that first ball off the tee. Most golfers begin every new golf year by thinking "This is the year!" Ashley and Parsons began their meeting by talking for a good five minutes about their golf games. It's something golfers particularly enjoy especially at this time of year.

"Frank," said Ashley, "I told you I had a few thoughts about this committee job you've taken on, and again, I thank you for accepting. I might as well tell you it isn't going to be easy. Our old building is beginning to show its age. Water leaks from the roof into the main dining room, and the wallpaper is faded and water-stained. God knows what's behind the walls, plumbing problems at the very least. The rest rooms are a mess, and we have three kitchens, one of which is not busy about 95 percent of the time. We do pretty good business in the grills, but our banquet volume is falling every month and every year. We need that volume to help produce revenue and keep dues down. Bottom line: we've got lots of problems. The present board and past ones, sadly, have lacked the guts to look this situation straight in the face and take the right action. It's just like Congress and the national debt. It's a disgrace, and now the problem is worse than it was a year ago, and a year from now it will be worse yet.

"The ugly truth is the joint needs a major fixing. The physical structure is only part of it. The membership will be pretty much against anything we propose, and the whole issue will be very sticky, including the cost of any project we decide to tackle."

He paused and grinned at Parsons. "You wanna back out?"

Frank grinned back. "Nope, I said I'd do it, and I will. Hell, Chuck, I've been deeply involved in up-to-the-ass corporate stuff, I've worked with tough CEO's and miserable boards of directors, and even stockholders. Also franchisee groups who mostly can't think beyond tomorrow morning. You name it, I've seen it."

"I know," said Chuck Ashley. "That's the main reason I asked you to take on this job. But there's something else we haven't talked much about. And that's this asshole Chet Phillips. He's bad news, Frank. Worse than you think. He's a relentless, tenacious son of a bitch. He's gonna get even with me for what he sees as a slight at the annual meeting. He's gonna come after me, I know that. And when he makes his move, it'll be like nothing this Club has ever seen before.

"I know this in my bones. And it's not far away. I'm betting he's working on something right this minute!"

x x x x x x

In Chet Phillips's mail was a large, brown envelope. There was no return address. He tore it open. Inside was a thick file of paper. In his first very quick look at it, there were computer printouts, chits, and several memos and letters. There was a note clipped to the first page. The note was unsigned:

> Here's what I've been able to find so far. I hope it's what you want. Most of it explains itself, but I should point out one or two things. You'll find a separate group of chits with lines drawn through them. These are Mr. Ashley's. He does this when members of the board get together, for a board golf outing or a board lunch. The line drawn through means the Club picks up the bill, not the individual member. This amounts to a few hundred dollars a year. I don't know if Club rules permit this or not, but Mr. Ashley does do it.
> When the board plays golf together, as they do a couple of times a year, Mr. Ashley always has the Club pick up the expense for caddies, drinks, etc.
> There's one other thing. Several members of Mr. Ashley's family belong to this Club. They all work for Mr. Ashley's company, I think. Sometimes, when they sign chits, our office can't tell which Ashley it is, and sometimes they forget to put down their Club number. Most of the time, in fact. So Mr. Ashley has asked us to set up a single file for all Ashley chits and send one bill to him at his company. I don't know that there's anything wrong with this, but I thought you should know about it.

Phillips ran through the total file, making notes. He smiled to himself as he did so. There were dozens of chits in the file, a hundred or more. He looked at each one. He sat for a minute, then picked up the phone and called Esterbrook.

"This is your friend. I got the file. Wonderful! I have a couple of quick questions. I know Mr. Ashley was at one time chair of the Grounds Committee. I'd like you to go back and check his expense reports for that time. And two, I want you from now on to keep a close eye on what Mr. Frank Parsons does, particularly now that he's House Committee chairman."

"All right, Mr. Phillips, I...."

He interrupted her. "Marianne, never, never address me by name over the telephone! I've told you that!"

"Yes, sir, it was a slip of the tongue." She was suddenly terrified, but she knew she was in too deep now to get out.

"Sir, there's one more thing. I don't know how to say it, but the other day, I was walking by Mr. Branch's office, and he had Lillian Thompson in there and they were sort of whispering to each other, and he had his hands on her...on her shoulders and neck. I could not hear what they were saying."

"Jesus Christ!" Chet Phillips clapped his hands together.

26

Chapter Ten

Claude Branch

In the few years that he had been manager of Pheasant Ridge, Claude Branch had regular meetings with his full staff. This in itself was not unusual, but the way he conducted the meetings was.

First, the meetings were not held in the Club offices, but in the main lounge where normally members gathered. Second, each meeting was chaired by a different staff member. And third, Branch seldom spoke except for an occasional reaction to a question or comment. His managerial style was much appreciated by his people. One of the results of this kind of meeting was far less internal strife than is present at many country clubs. Few Pheasant Ridge members knew about this particular skill of Branch and its positive affect on the total operation.

Holding the meetings in the lounge was a positive tactic. The meetings took place early morning before any member was likely to be around. They were fast paced. Each staff chair set his or her own agenda and there were no limits on what could be discussed. When this kind of meeting was first tried, staff people were hesitant to speak, not understanding the objective and suspecting some kind of trick. Gradually, however, over a period of three years they came to look forward to the meetings, and most of them spoke their minds. As a key employee, Marianne Esterbrook came to all the meetings, but seldom spoke. Now, in her new role as spy for Phillips, she began to carefully observe everything that went on. And after the meetings, she made notes on what certain employees said.

On this particular morning, there was a spirited discussion as to whether employees should get free meals during working hours. It was a subject Branch himself had opened up more than a year ago, and then he let it stay quiet. Branch had felt, early on, that employees would feel the free food was their basic right. He had never said so, and his views on the subject were not known. In the early days of the Club, free meals would have been out of the question as a fiscally careful board knew the expense would not be looked at kindly by the membership. As the years went by and America's corporations began making more and more concessions to employees, the subject of free meals was not controversial. Many clubs in the U.S. did so, and Pheasant Ridge had tried it, then discontinued it, then tried it again. The board had no strong feelings on the matter, and felt that Branch was in a far better position to make a recommendation than any of them.

At 9 A.M., the time agreed upon for ending the meeting, the discussion was still going on. Though he did not say so, Branch was delighted that many staff members felt that free meals were not something they had a right to expect. Most of them thought that meals should be theirs at cost.

27

Only a few felt free meals during working hours were part of a basic employee benefit package. Branch felt it had been a fine meeting, and he told them a vote on the subject would be taken at the next meeting. Based on that vote, he said, he would make a recommendation to the board.

As the meeting broke up, one young woman approached Branch with a question. She was, she said, almost eight months pregnant, and asked about the Club policy on leave time. Branch had been expecting the question and knew that the young woman would bring the matter up as her pregnancy progressed. Many clubs, of course, have a written policy on such matters. Pheasant Ridge, to date, had not. Branch was allowed to judge each case individually, but he also knew that sooner or later a set policy would have to be put in place.

Branch was a fundamentally warm person, even though the membership did not see him that way. He liked the young woman and was happy about the fact she would soon give birth.

He said now, "Julie, it's wonderful you're about to have your baby. I think you know my wife Pam is also expecting, and I think you're on about the same timetable. First of all, you certainly can plan on taking your time to recover and you come back when you feel it's right to do so. I know you'll use good judgement. You're a fine employee, and we want you to not feel any pressure."

The girl beamed at him. "Thank you, Mr. Branch. I want you to know my husband and I both feel you're a good man to work for and that Pheasant Ridge is a nice place to be."

Branch was truly moved, and in his enthusiasm and affection for the girl, he impulsively reached out and put his hand on her stomach.

"Golly," he said, "you feel about the same way my wife does."

She was momentarily startled, but quickly realized it was a gesture of sincere affection and smiled at him. The incident had taken but a few seconds, and few in the room even noticed it. One person, however, did. Marianne Esterbrook, a few feet away, made an immediate mental note of what had taken place, and later wrote it down and placed the paper in her file.

Chapter Eleven

House Committee Meeting

Parsons had selected the people he wanted on his House Committee: four men and three women. He knew that some committees of the Club had as many as ten members or more, but he did not like large committees. His business experience over many years had taught him that no more than two or three committee appointments ever make a real contribution. He wanted people he could work with who cared about the Club, and people who would come regularly to meetings and come on time.

He picked a date on his personal calendar and called Lillian Thompson, asking her to get out a notice to each person of the time and place: 5:15 P.M. in the Governor's Room. He also informed Branch, saying he wanted the manager at all meetings. He did this not only because he knew Branch was familiar with the building's structural problems, but it was important that Branch feel wanted.

Branch suggested that the Club's chief engineer should also be present at all meetings.

"Nobody knows this old place like Billy Gomez," he told Parsons. "You'll find him invaluable."

"Fine," Frank said. "I know him a little, and I like him. He seems to really care about this place."

For the first meeting, Parsons had prepared a written agenda, which was copied in advance to each member. Running a meeting was something he did very well. His meetings started on time and ended on time. His normal business practice was to not permit meaningless conversation on unimportant items, but he knew he could not operate that way with volunteers. He structured his agenda so that any member could bring up any subject in the final fifteen minutes of a committee meeting.

One of his primary objectives was to have members understand that he ran tight meetings, and tight meetings started on time and moved along briskly. At exactly 5:15 with but two committee members present, he started the meeting.

Branch said, "Mr. Parsons, there are still five committee members not present."

"I know that, Claude, but my meetings start on time, and we may as well establish that point right now. I realize all these people are volunteers, but so am I, and so are the two people who are here. We've got a huge job ahead of us, and we've got to be businesslike. If we establish this discipline right now at our first meeting, people will pretty quickly get the idea. Frankly, I don't like people straggling in many minutes after a meeting has started and I hate the waste of time going back over items they have missed."

"Yes, sir," said Branch, making a mental note to always be on time for a Frank Parsons meeting.

As Parsons began to talk, two committee members walked in, obviously surprised the meeting was already under way. He said nothing to them, did not acknowledge them and continued with what he was saying. It was obvious to one member who knew him well that Parsons was irritated and would likely say something sooner or later.

Parsons continued "In a few minutes I'm going to ask Mr. Gomez, who is our chief engineer, to talk about the condition of our building. His remarks are most pertinent because keeping this old place up is a key part of our responsibility. Not only must we not allow it to deteriorate further than it already has, but I want to present to the board within one month our recommendations for two plans, one short-range, the other long. I doubt anyone here, with the exception of Mr. Branch, knows what the condition of this building is really like. Only in the past week or so have I learned myself about some of the problems. I've had my eyes opened.

"There are two reasons, or two key ones, why we cannot let this building continue to go downhill. One is obviously the fact that it will cost more and more to operate, given certain structural problems. I'm talking about such things as air conditioning, heating, water seepage in lots of places, and nearly critical flooding conditions in parts of the men's locker room. And I emphasize to you that those I've mentioned are only a few items of many that need our attention. The second reason is that from a marketing standpoint, this building is probably hurting us far more than we appreciate."

One woman raised her hand. "Mr. Parsons, ah, Frank, you used the word `marketing' just now. What did you mean by that?"

"Okay, good question. We may not realize it, but we have to do a far better job of marketing this Club, that is, looking at it the way a business organization would. In business, you never stand still; you either go forward or you go backward. And if you don't constantly improve and upgrade your `product,' you will only go one way—and that's backward."

One of the committee members, a businessman, nodded approvingly.

Parsons continued "When I use the word `marketing,' I do so because as a Club we must realize we are in competition. In competition with other Clubs in the area, with restaurants, hotels, sports clubs, and other social organizations. We must see to it that not only are we competitive but ahead of the others. Ahead of them in food, in service, in facilities. It means we must have ideas and events that will keep our members coming to us week after week, month after month. I assure you, `marketing' is not a word I use lightly."

"Well," said the woman, "You're the chairman and you know what you want to accomplish, but I would hate to see us start to look at Pheasant Ridge as a `business.' And I don't think of us in any competition. After all, we're Pheasant Ridge!"

Frank smiled. "Well, we can certainly disagree. But I have looked at the figures, and our banquet business is going steadily down. That's because our facilities have slipped. Our food is still excellent and there's nothing wrong with our service, but the building itself is hurting us badly. What is the first question we are asked when someone considers us for a banquet venue?"

He paused and looked around the room. "Okay, I'll tell you. The first or second question someone looking for a place to throw a big party asks us is `Do you have handicapped facilities?' Obviously, we don't. There is only one bathroom in the whole place that can be used by a handicapped person and that is in the men's locker room. What does a female guest do if she has to use the bathroom and she is handicapped?"

Again he looked around the room.

"Claude, how many banquets have we lost out on because we have no handicapped facilities?"

Branch paused for a moment. "Well, I know for sure we lost one yesterday because of that. We lost a big wedding reception by one of our own members because someone in the bridal party was handicapped. I'd say we lose at least a couple a month, probably more than that because I'm not always told by the receptionist or our catering manager. These events mean thousands of dollars to us, Mr. Parsons."

"Thank you. I was here the other day when a woman was walking through the lounge with our catering manager. She was checking us out for a big party in a couple of months. I listened to her. She pointed out the frayed carpet in the lounge, and she asked about our chairs, some of which look like they've gone through a war. She spotted some water damage on the wallpaper. I looked at the place through her eyes, and it looked pretty bad!"

The woman did not look convinced. She said, "I was listening to Chet Phillips, that is, Mr. Phillips, the other day. He said there is one reason people want to join this Club, and that's the golf course. He thinks spending a lot of money on this building is dumb. Oh, he'd fix it up here and there, but no big remodeling job."

"Well, that's where Mr. Phillips and I disagree. And I don't know what is meant by `fixing it up here and there.' That philosophy has prevailed for far too long, and that's why we're in the situation we're in now. That's the way our government in Washington has treated Social Security for many years. And now Social Security is close to a major disaster, and so is this building!

"The truth is," he continued, now with some anger, "we've got to start looking at this Club in a different way. We are no longer in the same situation we were in just five short years ago. We are no longer just a golf club for men. We are a Club for families. More and more the `family' is coming into play. We've got to make this place a wonderfully attractive place for the entire family. That's marketing!"

"Well," said the woman. "I agree that a Club should not be just a place for men. But I don't know whether I'd go as far as you seem to want to go. And I can tell you this—you and Mr. Phillips are going to clash over this issue."

Parsons did not smile. "I'm sure you're right. But Chet Phillips, in my view, represents an attitude that should no longer prevail."

The woman stared him. "Well, I'll see what Mr. Phillips says about that!"

"Fine," said Parsons.

To himself he said *Oh, shit.*

The meeting continued until the time he had set for suggestions by members of the committee. There were two thoughts introduced. Neither was particularly significant and there was no discussion. Parsons then said, "Our meeting is close to ending, but I'd like to comment on one point I feel to be important. I hope you will not be offended by what I say. Our meeting today was scheduled for 5:15, and it is a strong belief of mine that meetings should start on time. At that time, 5:15, there were just two committee members here, but I started anyway. I have learned from years in

31

business that a meeting which does not start on time is already on its way to being a bad meeting.

"I realize we are all volunteers, but in accepting membership on the House Committee, I'm assuming you believe our job is important. So we're going to always start on time, and I make the firm commitment to you that we'll end on time. You will be able to tell your family or anyone else what time you'll be through here. I think that's important, just as important as starting on time.

"I hope you agree with this, and I'll say nothing more about it. Thank you for coming. You'll be notified soon about our next meeting and again, as today, you'll get an agenda."

At first, no one said anything, but then one of the men spoke, "Frank, I agree with your meeting policy. I was late today because in all other committee meetings I've attended over the years here, no chairman ever started on time, so I just said to myself 'what the hell!' I regret that, and you have my assurance I will be on time from now on."

Parsons smiled. "Thank you." Two others then said pretty much the same thing.

Immediately after the meetings, as they were walking out, Claude Branch touched Parsons on the shoulder.

"Talk to you a minute, sir?"

"Sure, Claude. Shoot."

"Well, I thought your first meeting went pretty well. I'm glad you told them you expected meetings to start on time. I'm supposed to attend most committee meetings around here, and I can tell you none of them start on time. Ever.

"Mr. Parsons, it's none of my business, and maybe I shouldn't ask, but how did you happen to ask Laura Carter to be on the committee?"

"Funny you should ask, Claude. I don't really know her; she's the only committee member I don't really know at all. Well, I had heard she was really into Club activity and would work hard. So I called her. It's that simple."

"Are you aware, Mr. Parsons, that she and her husband are very tight with Chet Phillips? Mr. Phillips, I mean?

"No, I didn't know that. Oh, and also, someone recommended her. Let's see, who the heck was it?"

Branch smiled. "Could it have been Mr. Bradley? Louis Bradley?"

"Lou Bradley? Yeah, I think it was. Yeah, he caught me in the grill one day. Said she'd be a great committee member."

Again Branch smiled. He liked this man Parsons. He wanted him to do well. And, he sensed in Parsons a man who could be a real ally in case down the line he might need some solid support.

He said, "Again, I probably shouldn't say this, but now I'm into it, I'm going to tell you that if you'd asked me I would have recommended against Mrs. Carter. She's, well, I know her. And I guarantee Mr. Phillips will be hearing about what you said within the hour."

"Well, thanks, Claude, I appreciate your concern. But I'm a pretty tough dude, and Mrs. Carter doesn't scare me. Neither does Chet Phillips."

"Yes, sir. Anyway, one more thing, Mr. Parsons. I noticed you signed for the beverages we had in the meeting. That's not necessary. Beverage during committee meetings are on the Club."

Branch walked back toward the table on which the chit still lay. He drew a line through the middle of the bill.

"That means it's not valid. You won't get billed for it, sir."

Chapter Twelve

Laura Carter

"Chet, it's Laura Carter. I've just come from a meeting of the new House Committee. This man Parsons is chair, did you know that?"

"Yeah, Laura, I did. Why? What's up?"

"Well, he said he disagreed with you about the golf course. And about the clubhouse. He said you no longer counted. He said the clubhouse is more important than the golf course! He talked about `marketing' the Club. My God, the things he said!"

"Wait a minute, Laura, slow down. You're sure he said the golf course isn't important? He's a smart guy, I can't believe he said that. Are you really sure?"

"Well, he said something like that. Yes, I'm sure. I thought you'd want to know."

"I do, Laura, I do. Thanks for telling me. I guess this is happening faster than I thought it would. You're absolutely sure he said the course isn't important?"

"Yes, I'm sure."

She hung up. For a few seconds she sat and wondered if she had really heard Frank Parsons say what she said he had. *Oh, well*, she thought, *that was about what he had said.*

Chapter Thirteen

Pulling the Trigger

The phone on Phillips's desk rang while he was standing at his office door.
"Yes?"

"Mr. Phillips—oh, I'm sorry, sir. Slip of the tongue. I know you don't want me to say your name."

"That's right, Marianne. It's very important that no one knows you're contacting me. Anyway, what's up?"

"Well, sir, a chit just arrived on my desk. It was signed by Mr. Parsons yesterday. But there's a line through it. That means he won't get billed for the drinks he ordered. About $15 worth. Thought you'd want to know."

"I do, Marianne. Thank you. Fifteen dollars worth of drinks and he got 'em free?"

"That's right, sir."

He put down the phone and made a note on his yellow pad. Out loud, he said, "Okay, folks, it's about time to pull the trigger."

Frank Parsons's phone rang. "Mr. Parsons, it's Claude Branch."

"Yes, Claude?"

"Mr. Parsons, I didn't tell you this yesterday, or last evening rather. But I guess I think you should know. Maybe you do know. Mr. Phillips is after me. He wants me fired. The man really hates me, I'm not sure why."

"Claude, I have been told something like this. Not that he hates you, but that he would prefer a new manager, probably one of his own choosing. I doubt that will happen. But why the call? Has something happened?"

"Well, yes. Mr. Phillips was just here in the Club office. He stopped in my doorway and just stood there for a minute, kind of sneering at me. Then he said, "How come you're here? Aren't you usually still at home this time of day?' Then he walked away, but then turned and came back. And this time he said—loud enough for everyone in the office to hear—'what's your work week these days—twenty, twenty-five hours? What goes around comes around, you know.' And he laughed one of those laughs of his and he walked out."

"Claude, first of all I'm sorry. And ashamed, on behalf of the Club. Is that it? Are you telling me everything that happened? Everything he said?"

"Yes, sir, that's exactly what he said. Mr. Parsons, I'm leveling with you, believe me."

"I do believe you, Claude. Thanks for calling me. And hang in there."

"Thanks, sir, I'll try."

The phone conversation over, Branch sat there. He noticed his hands.

They were shaking. He felt perspiration on his forehead.

Chet Phillips called Marianne Esterbrook later the same day.

"Marianne, it's your friend. Tell me, when Claude Branch went to the Club manager's meeting in Indianapolis, where did he stay?"

"You mean what hotel?"

"That's what I mean. We paid for that trip, right? I mean we sent him to the meeting?"

"Yes, sir, well I don't know for sure, but I would assume it was Club business. We paid for it. I remember signing the check."

"Okay, Marianne, now listen. I want you to get his expense report for attending those meetings. And I want you to get from the hotel a print-out of his expenses, his phone calls, everything you can get your hands on. Got that?"

"Yes, sir. It will take me a few days, I'd think."

Five minutes later, Esterbrook's phone rang again.

"It's your friend again. I just thought of something. Have you noticed Mr. Branch doing any more neck massaging or anything like that? Anything. Anything at all."

"Well, not really. He does pat people on the back occasionally. That's the way he is."

"You mean he pats women office workers on the back?"

"Yes, sometimes he does that."

"Thank you, Marianne."

Chapter Fourteen

The First Letter

Pheasant Ridge board meetings were usually held once a month, total of twelve a year. The Club president always had the authority to call a special meeting if he felt it necessary. Special meetings were not rare because at a modern-day country club, there will almost always be a situation that calls for an immediate or emergency meeting.

In calling a special meeting as the golf season was getting under way, Ashley saw a critical need for a thorough discussion before the entire membership had returned. In this case, he felt the need was so urgent that he had Lillian Thompson call out-of- town board members asking them to make a special trip back to town. The Club would pay the expense. One board member was not available because he was on a world cruise, but all others would come back.

No member had been told the reason for the meeting, but they all had great respect for Ashley and knew he would not call a special meeting without feeling a real need. Well before the time of the meeting, 6 P.M., each man was in the Governor's Room and seated. There was little small talk, and no laughter. At six Ashley walked in, unsmiling, with none of his customary warmth. He sat down.

"Mr. Secretary, do we have a quorum?"

"Yes, Mr. President," said Larry Costello.

"Thank you. I declare this an official meeting of the board of governors of Pheasant Ridge. Mr. Secretary, I ask that you take minutes.

"Gentlemen, I have in my hand a letter from a member of this Club. The letter was delivered to my office three days ago, certified mail. The letter, which I will read, contains a serious, serious—very serious—and I stress the word serious—accusation against our Club manager, Mr. Claude Branch."

The members now noticed for the first time that Branch, who usually attended every board meeting, was absent.

Ashley continued, "I say to you that this matter is completely confidential. It must not be discussed outside this room. As I've said, the matter is deadly serious. Mr. Branch has been accused of improper sexual advances against various staff employees. At the very least, it appears we may face—as a Club—sexual harassment charges. If true, this can mean a huge fine and surely would involve expensive legal fees to defend ourselves. The charges, or allegations, I should say, are potentially very damaging.

"The letter I refer to was written by Chet Phillips. It is addressed to me, as Club president. It demands that we fire Branch. Now. Today. I tell you in advance the letter is not very well-written, and there are words occasionally spelled incorrectly. But its meaning is very clear."

Dear President Ashley.

For some time, as you know, I have been pointing out flaws in the performance of our manager, Mr. Branch. I have said he is unprofessional, lazy, and not on top of his responsibility as manager. We are a quality country club, one of the finest in America. And we have a third rate manager, if that.

He is unpopular with all of the members of his staff. None of the waiters and waitresses like him, he doesn't get along with our golf professional, and he runs a terrible operation overall.

I have told you this before, but you have refused—"failed" is a better word—to take any action. I now have information that Mr. Branch has sexually touched two or more members of our female staff.I have a witness who will so testify. For all I know, Branch has probably touched other women. He's that kind of man and not fit to be here. I don't know why he is here.He must have something on you, Mr. Ashley.

I also have information that our grill manager, Mr. Russell Manders, uses foul language with our kitchen personnel and has on occasion stole food from our supplies. I have a witness to this too.

I also have reason to believe Manders is a queer and that he hangs out with known fags and has employed in the past at least two damn fags in our kitchen and waiter staff.

I demand, as of this letter, that you terminate Mr. Branch and Mr. Manders immediately. I also remind you that more than a month ago I demanded that you change the way the executive committee is elected. I gave you one week to get back to me, and you have now used up lots more than that. Now I understand you have pulled your usual fast one and have allowed the present officer group to stay in place. This will not be allowed.

Unless you follow through on all this stuff, I intend to take steps to see that you do.

Sincerely,
Chester W. Phillips

Ashley put the letter down, his fingers trembling.

"Okay, guys, there you got it."

"That son of a bitch!" said Larry Costello. Other board members reacted in kind. The room was suddenly filled with the voices of four or five men all trying to speak at the same time.

"Okay," said Ashley, "one at a time. Hold your hand up and I'll recognize you. Anyone who wants to speak can, if we have to stay here all night. Larry, you reacted first, and since you're an executive committee member and in the direct line of fire, and an attorney, I guess we should get your take on this."

"Well," began the Club Secretary, "In the first place, we shouldn't be surprised. This is vintage Chet Phillips, although this is the first time he's gone so far. Second, we must take him seriously. We all know he's relentless, and I would guess he's contacted an attorney. Third, clearly we do not take any kind of action until we know the facts. We must find out if the charges of sexual harassment are valid. Do we know who the women are, Chuck?"

"No we don't. Larry, I've done nothing on this. Nothing. I was waiting for this meeting. You guys are the only ones who know."

"Okay," said Costello, "Our first job, and we've got to do it fast, is find out who the two women are and then hear what they've got to say. Legally, guys, the courts have been pretty vague about what sexual harassment is. It's often been left up to the individual judge. From where I sit, this is Chet Phillips's opening gun in a vengeful campaign to make major changes in this Club. Next he probably will go after us specifically, certainly the executive committee as well as individual board members. I anticipate he will follow up this letter with another, a blockbuster, about a week from now. Oh, say, Chuck, do you know who his mole might be in the office?"

Ashley said, "I think I might. It's probably our comptroller, gal named Marianne Esterbrook. She knows everything, she runs our money operation, and she dislikes almost everybody. I'll check that out tomorrow."

Costello continued. "I'm not an attorney who specializes in employment problems, but I know a couple who do. And there's one in my building who's a nationally known authority on sexual harassment. If we hire him on this matter, he won't be cheap, I promise you. In fact, guys, this whole damn thing is gonna end up costing us a bunch. You can bet on that. So, Chuck, if you want, I'll find us a legal expert and get him in here whenever you can meet with him."

Frank Parsons raised his hand. "Guys, this whole thing amazes me. I thought I'd seen everything. Obviously, I'm a babe in the woods. But I see one ray of light at the moment, just to make us all feel better. First, Phillips may easily paint himself into a lawsuit here. He's accused, in writing, a member of our staff of stealing. And he's used language that I don't think would be acceptable in a courtroom. As chair of the House Committee, let me check out where Phillips got his information about Manders. I can do that without causing a fuss."

After hearing more comments, Ashley decided the matter had gone as far as it could for the moment. He asked for a motion to adjourn.

Chapter Fifteen

The Moles

The next day Costello called Chuck Ashley. "Chuck, I've found an attorney who specializes in employee problems, and he's even more of a specialist in sexual harassment situations."

"Good, when can we meet with him?"

"Tomorrow at 11 A.M. His office in the Antwell Building," fourth floor.

"Good. See you there."

Also on the second day, the morning after the meeting, Parsons called Russell Manders, the grill manager. "Russ, I need to see you today as soon as possible. Are you available?"

"Yes, Mr. Parsons. Anytime today. I've got lots to do, except for the noon lunch period, I can see you anytime. What's up? Should I prepare for anything? You need some figures? Or what?"

"No, Russ, you need do nothing. I'll be there at 2:30. I'll come to your office."

Following the call from Costello, Chuck Ashley called Thompson in the Club offices.

"Lillian, this is Mr. Ashley. I'd like to see you today soon as possible. Any chance we could meet around 5 this afternoon?"

"Yes, sir, Mr. Ashley, whenever you wish. Where do you wish to meet?"

"Well, not in the Club office. Do you have a car? Is it in the employee's parking area?"

"Yes, it is. It's a 1994 Honda coupe."

"All right, fine. I'll drive into the lot and park right next to your car. We can talk right there."

x x x x x x

The following day at 11 A.M. Ashley walked into the fourth floor offices of Kramer and Morrissey, one of the city's largest law firms. Costello was in the lobby area. Together they were walked to the office of one of the firm's young attorneys.

The discussion lasted two hours, right through lunch. The attorney, Richard Kassel, did most of the talking. The three men agreed on what was to be done next. Ashley felt very comfortable with the youthful lawyer.

x x x x x x

At 2:30 P.M. the preceding day Parsons walked up to the door of the small office used by Russ Manders. He had come to know the grill manager fairly well. He liked him. Manders had come to the Club from one of the popular restaurants in the city. He knew the restaurant business and was very good with members of the Club. He had grown up in a middle-class section of town, part of a blue-collar family. His father was a union steward, his mother a housekeeper. He was street smart, very knowledgeable about sports, a no-nonsense young man. Parsons found it very hard to believe what Chet Phillips had said about him.

Manders stood up, and the two men shook hands. "Mr. Parsons, come on in and have a seat. It's not much, but it's all I've got." He smiled but he was obviously nervous. Instinct told him this was not a casual visit by the House Committee chair.

Frank said, "I'll get right to the point. But I caution you, Russ, this conversation is off the record. You are not to repeat anything we talk about. I'm dead serious."

"Yes, sir, you can trust me."

Parsons knew he could. "Russ, what I want to talk about is serious, but I don't want you to be nervous. I know that's easy for me to say." He grinned at Manders and saw the man relax a little.

"Russ, there are things I can't tell you and some things I can. One of our members is causing a problem. I can't tell you who it is, and I can't tell you much about it. However, this member says there is thievery going on in the kitchen area. What do you know about that?"

Manders looked straight at him. "Mr. Parsons, I think I know about that. Some time ago, one of our kitchen workers was having a party at his home and he took some pies, leftover pies, that had not been eaten that day. We usually sell such stuff to the staff at cost. He took four pies and he told me about it. I forgot, quite frankly. He should have been billed. It's my fault. He's a good man, one of our best."

"Okay," said Parsons. "Good. Anything else?"

"Not that I can think of. Oh, wait a minute. I took some pot pies home for my folk's Christmas. That was in December. I am positive I paid for those pies with a check to Marianne Esterbrook. I've got my check book right here. Let's see, December 22. There's the notation of the check I wrote."

Manders looked at Parsons. His look was one of growing anger.

"Mr. Parsons, who said I stole something from the Club? I think I know. Was it Marianne Esterbrook?"

Parsons said, "Russ, I can't tell you. Trust me. Is there anything else on this subject?"

"Not that I can think of. Oh, I wouldn't doubt at all that some of our people indulge in small, petty stuff from time to time. It happens, no way to really check it. It used to happen at the Parrot, where I worked before. It's part of the business, like bar tenders cheating a little all the time. I don't like it, but frankly I don't get too excited about it. Mr. Parsons, if you want, I'll talk to the staff, make them know we're paying attention."

"Okay, Russ, that's probably a good idea. But don't make a big deal out of it. It's important this not become an issue. I trust you to do this without a fuss. I don't want to hear any rumors floating about theft in the Club."

Both men knew, however, that no matter how discreetly Russ Manders handled any communication with staff people, the word would leak out.

Parsons did not mention the other part of Chet Phillips's accusation against Russell Manders. He did not believe it, and he'd be damned if he'd lower himself to the level of Chet Phillips.

x x x x x x

At a little after five in the afternoon, Ashley pulled his car up along-side of the red Honda coupe in the employee parking area. It was still light. At this time of year, sunset would not take place until well after six. Chuck Ashley hoped no one would see him sitting in the front seat of Lillian Thompson's car.

He opened the door of the Honda and got in. Lillian said, her voice betraying her nervousness, "Good afternoon, Mr. Ashley." She was afraid to say more.

"Lillian, please don't be nervous or afraid," he began. "But it is important that I talk to you. And be aware this conversation is confidential. Please don't say anything to anyone, even your husband. There is no way I can be anything but direct in what I am going to ask you. Have you been, ah, sexually harassed by anyone in the Club office? Has any employee you know been sexually harassed? There, I said it." He found himself relieved that the words had come out.

Thompson's face was first red and then slowly turned white. Her hands trembled. Ashley made a try at calming her. "Lillian, please don't be afraid. There's nothing wrong, at least nothing you need to concern yourself about. But I do, we do, that is, need to know."

The woman made a try at calming herself. "Mr. Ashley, I know of no sexual harassment in our office. No, I have not been sexually harassed in any way. You must believe that. And if some women on our staff had been, I know I would know about it."

Ashley, vastly relieved, asked his next question. "All right. Good. Now think about this. Has anything happened— anything at all—that someone might have misinterpreted? I'm talking about things that might seem harmless but seen in the wrong way might look like harassment?"

"No, sir. Nothing. Oh, wait a minute. Oh my God! It couldn't be!" She put a hand to her face in obvious distress.

Ashley waited. He said nothing. He hoped the look on his face told her nothing.

"Mr. Ashley, this is terrible! If what this is, well, if what happened has caused these questions, I am shocked. Some weeks back, I'm not sure when, I had a stiff neck. I was in Mr. Branch's office near the end of the day. It had been a tough day, and I sometimes get this neck problem after a long workday and extra stress. Mr. Branch massaged my neck for a minute or two. It helped a lot. I can't imagine anyone seeing that as sexual harassment."

She sat a moment, then said, "Oh, my God, I'll bet someone walked by Mr. Branch's office at that moment. I think I can remember who it was, although I didn't think anything at the time."

"Who walked by, Lillian? It's important that I know."

"Why, it was Marianne Esterbrook. That's who it had to be. Did she tell you?"

"No, Lillian, that's all I can say, she didn't tell me. Anything else you want to say?"

"No sir. But that Marianne. This sounds just like her. Goddamn her! Always trying to make trouble. I'm sorry, Mr. Ashley."

"No problem, Lillian. Well, thank you. Let me know if you think of anything else. And remember, not a word to anyone about this." He went

41

back to his car and drove out of the lot.

Lillian Thompson, badly shaken, drove home. She had not intended to tell her husband. But it did slip out. The whole conversation.

x x x x x

Parsons picked up his phone at the first ring.

"Mr. Parsons, this is Russ Manders. You didn't ask, but I can tell you who on our restaurant staff has put out that information about, well, what we talked about. I know it was a person named Gert. Gertrude Carlson. She's been here a long time, but she really isn't very good. I don't trust her and neither does anybody else. She's a whiner and complainer and spends a lot of her time out in the dining area talking to members. And that's not her job."

Parsons said, "Are you sure? Or are you just guessing?"

"I'm sure. Oh, what the hell, the reason I know is I asked her. And she immediately acknowledged she had spoken to Mr. Phillips. And then she made a comment along the lines of `You'll get what's coming to you, Mr. Manders.'"

"She said that?"

"She sure did. And I'll tell you something else as long as I'm spilling my guts to you, Mr. Parsons. Gert is tight with Marianne Esterbrook. What does that tell you?"

"I guess it tells me something is going on that is just getting started. Thanks, Russ, that's all I can say right now."

He put the phone down. So now he knew who the two moles were, one in the Club office, another in the kitchen. *My God*, he thought to himself. *I wonder if there's one in the pro shop.*

x x x x x

"Larry, Chuck Ashley. I've found out about the sexual harassment. Part of it, anyway. Lillian Thompson had her neck massaged by her boss a while back. Marianne Esterbrook saw it happen and obviously told that bastard Chet Phillips. She flatly denies any sexual harassment. She likes her boss, always has.

"I've also found out the other woman, the other one who Phillips claimed was harassed. It was, or rather is, a young, pregnant girl in the office. She's about eight months along. At an office gathering a while back, in a conversation about pregnancy, Branch apparently touched her stomach. Very lightly. And he made some comment about his wife being the same condition. All pretty harmless. He was stupid to do that, but from everything I can find out, he meant no harm and the girl herself says he didn't harass her. She's prepared to say that if it becomes necessary somewhere down the line."

"That's good going, Chuck. I feel a lot better. We'd better get back to the attorney. Want me to call him? Oh, and by the way, touching that young woman was pretty stupid, and Branch ought to know better. You should talk to him about it."

"Larry, I already have. Well, anyway, now we know the players, so let's go see your lawyer guy again. With his hourly rate of $150, this is gonna cost the Club, I can see that. I've got a hunch this is just barely the beginning."

42

"Chuck, this is Frank Parsons. I now know who the mole in the kitchen is. It's a woman named Gert. Gertrude Carlson. You know her?"

"Not really. How'd you find out?"

"Had a good meeting with Russ Manders. He's got a solid explanation for the business of stealing from the kitchen. Looks like a false alarm."

Chapter Sixteen

Richard Kassel

Larry Costello noted on his calendar that the Club was now well past the deadline date Phillips had specified. He took mild pleasure from this fact. He had not allowed himself to be intimidated by Phillips' demands, and he had no personal timetable for checking into the allegations. By nature, however, he was not one to let things slide. He knew that Phillips was surely at work on his own schedule. And his instinct told him that not many days would go by until Phillips made his next move. He was pretty sure it would be a second letter.

Richard Kassel, the attorney who had first met with Ashley and Costello, was again with the two men in his downtown office.

"First, I can tell you with confidence that if what happened to these two women is what you've told me, it is not sexual harassment. And the fact their neither woman looks at what happened as sexual in nature further strengthens my opinion. Mr. Phillips is way off base. Unless, and I stress this word, there is something none of us knows about. What is your feeling about that?"

Ashley said, "I have every confidence these are the two women Phillips was talking about. I suppose there's always the chance that others are involved, but I seriously doubt it."

"Okay," said the attorney. "Do I have your permission to speak to the two women myself?"

"You do," said Ashley.

"Anything else?" said Kassel, a man who moved quickly and decisively.

"One thing," Costello said softly. "I would bet a thousand bucks that Phillips has got something going right now. No way of telling what it is, but that guy, as we all know, is relentless."

Ashley nodded. And Kassel, who was just beginning to get a feeling for their mutual adversary, shrugged his shoulders. "It is always possible, gentlemen, that once he gets a whiff of some strong opposition to his tactics, he'll back off."

Ashley and Costello looked at each other without speaking.

x x x x x x

Marianne Esterbrook's phone rang in her office.

"This is your friend. Got anything new for me?"

"I might have, sir. There was a man in the office today and he talked to Lillian Thompson for some time. They were in a room with the door closed. He also talked to Julie, the girl who is pregnant. Then he went into Mr. Branch's office and was in there for about an hour. He looked like a

44

lawyer."

"He looked like a lawyer? How does a lawyer look?"

"I don't know, sir. He had on a dark suit, and I just had that feeling."

"Well, you may be right. Anything else?"

"I'm not sure. While he was talking to Lillian at first before the door closed, they turned and both looked in the direction of my office. I didn't hear what they said. I'm kind of scared, sir."

"Don't be," said Phillips. "You've done nothing wrong. What you're doing is right. Hang in there."

He hung up and said to himself So they've got a lawyer, huh? Okay, I have, too.

x x x x x x

Richard Kassel spent two hours reading the bylaws of Pheasant Ridge Country Club. He made several pages of notes. When he finished, he dialed the Club number and asked for Esterbrook.

"Ms. Esterbrook, you don't know me. My name is Richard Kassel. I'm an attorney. I'd like to see you this afternoon. In your office."

"What about, Mr., is it Kassel?"

"Yes, that's it. I'll tell you what it's about when we meet."

"I'm pretty busy, Mr. Kassel. I have lots to do."

"Ms. Esterbrook, this is important. It's Club business. You may take time away from your office duties."

"Mr. Kassel, I will have to get permission from Mr. Branch. He's my boss."

"Ms. Esterbrook, that will not be necessary. I will be there at 2 P.M. I will expect you to be available at that time."

Esterbrook, terrified, called Phillips.

"Sir, there's a lawyer coming to see me this afternoon. I tried to get out of it, but he was very firm. I'm very scared."

"Marianne, don't tell him anything. Nothing at all. Don't let him scare you. And if he threatens you, I want to know about it."

x x x x x x

At 4:30 the same afternoon, Kassel called Chuck Ashley.

"Well, I've talked with Esterbrook. She's your mole, all right. Broke down and cried. Told me how everyone hates her, everyone's against her. She told me she had given information, chits, and so on to Phillips. She talks to him frequently. And when she doesn't call him, he calls her. I asked her if she knew she was violating a specific bylaw of the Club. She didn't seem to know that. I did not threaten her—I know better than that— but I was pretty firm. I told her she was not to be in contact with Phillips any more."

In the very late afternoon, Esterbrook got a call. She was on her feet, ready to leave the office. She knew who it would be. She paused, thinking not to answer it. On the fifth ring she picked it up.

"This is your friend. What did the lawyer say? Who was he? Tell me!"

"Mr., ah, sir, I am not to talk with you again. He was very firm about that. This has to end, sir. I am getting into trouble."

"Marianne, goddammit, you're not in trouble. I've got a lawyer too. We'll protect you. You haven't done anything wrong."

"Well, sir he says I have. He says the bylaws do not permit what I've

45

been doing, talking to you, telling you things. It's nice that you want to protect me, but I must stop doing this. I don't want you to call me anymore."

She put down the phone. She was in tears. Her makeup was ruined. She sat down at her desk to repair her face. When she was through, she began to cry again. Then she got up, went to her car and drove home. She cried through most of the evening.

Chapter Seventeen

The Second Letter

Mail was delivered to Parson's home about eleven each morning. On this morning it was the usual advertisements, bills, and four personal letters. One envelope immediately caught his attention. There was no name on it, and the postmark was from a small town about twenty-five miles west of the city. On the outside of the envelope in large black type were the words:

"IF YOU LOVE PHEASANT RIDGE, YOU MUST READ THIS NOW!"

He ripped open the envelope. There were four pages. He checked the back page for a signature. There was none. But there were words where a signature would usually be: "THE WHISTLE BLOWER."
He went back to the first page and started reading:

> If you love Pheasant Ridge Country Club, it is critical that you read this entire letter. And then take the action indicated. There are lots of funny things going on at the Club you love, things that aren't good, things that are dishonest, things that are disgusting, things illegal and unethical.
>
> There are three people mostly responsible for all this dishonesty and sinister behavior. And if they are allowed to remain in place, the Club is doomed. These people are Claude Branch, the manager, Club President Charles Ashley, and Club Secretary Laurence Costello.
>
> These are the worst three, but there are others. One is board of governors member Frank Parsons, who is also chair of the powerful House Committee. Another is Grill Manager Russell Manders. Parsons, in the short time he has been House chair, has accepted special favors from the staff who give in to him because of his power. Manders is a thief, is known to have peculiar sexual orientation, and uses foul language in addressing people under him.
>
> I also charge the entire board of governors with dishonesty, particularly in their recent action with regard to the election of an Executive Committee.
>
> Further along in this letter, I will give you proof of everything I say here, proof that will lead you to only one conclusion: that we must immediately get rid of these sucking maggots and get this Club started on a long road to decency and good management.

The letter went on for three more pages. The grammar and language used got increasingly bad, and by the end of the last page it was clear to Frank that the words were coming from a person close to hysteria.

He put the letter down without finishing it. He sat for a full five minutes trying to organize his thoughts. He tried to let logic and reason overcome his considerable anger. The fact that Phillips's name was not at the end of the letter made no difference. The letter had been written by him.

Frank took a pen and pad of paper and made notes. He arrived after a few minutes at three points:

1. The letter was an all-out attack by a person who had now thrown all caution out the window and was on a mission.

2. A man of Phillips's shrewdness and intelligence would not have written such a letter without something that would appear to substantiate his charges.

3. A significant percentage of members would believe Phillips in spite of the fact they may not have liked him personally. These members would reason that he would not mail such a letter without proof.

Frank also noted that this affair would surely go on for some time and cause serious damage to the Club, no matter how it eventually turned out.

He said to himself: *We've got to go after this bastard and we can't waste any time. This is like a cancer.*

Throughout the day and evening, Parsons got calls from members and friends of his who wanted to know what was going on. Most of the men were familiar with the tactics of Chet Phillips. Their comments focused on what they felt was the key issue: Phillips was a known control freak and troublemaker. A few, however, seemed to believe parts of what had been written.

"After all," said one of these members, "he's got dates and details, and he seems to have proof."

Parsons, who at this point had not read the entire letter, was careful not to comment specifically. He thanked each member for his interest and urged him to stay calm and not jump to conclusions. His effort to this end was wasted, he knew, but he had to say it.

Although he had not read the entire letter because of his complete revulsion, he now eyeballed the pages until he found his name:

And now my accusations against board member and House Committee Chairman Mr. Frank Parsons. On four separate occasions Parsons, using the power of his chairmanship, has accepted free refreshments from the Club rather than signing the chits the way the rest of us ordinary members have to do. One of these chits was for $28.50. In his capacity as House chair, Parsons made the statement to his committee that "The golf course is not important to this Club." From this evidence, it should be obvious to all members that Mr. Parsons's ethics leave much to be desired and his statement about the golf course shows he is in no position to either be a board member or a committee chair.

As he read the paragraph, Frank's eyes grew narrow, and when he finished, he crumpled the page into a ball and threw it across the room.

"That son of a bitch!" he shouted.

On the same day Parsons got his copy of the letter, Esterbrook found in her mail an envelope with no return address on it. Inside was a check for $25 with a small typed note which read: "Hang in there." There was no name on the note and the check was a personal one signed by someone she did not know.

Mid-afternoon, Frank got a call from Ashley, asking him if he could attend a meeting of the executive committee at 7 P.M. He could.

It was an indication of the loyalty and integrity of the executive committee that on extremely short notice all members were at the meeting along with Parsons. Also present was a man he did not know, who was introduced to him as Attorney Richard Kassel.

Ashley was grim as he thanked each man for attending, and he formally identified Richard Kassel as the lawyer the Club had hired as its counsel in this matter.

"Guys," he said, "we were right about Chet Phillips. He's not just a loose cannon, I think he's probably mentally ill, and we've got to take some action. This thing is getting out of control, and we've got to do more than just sit still and take it. Frankly, guys, I've just about had it. What I would most like to do is go to Phillips's place and punch his lights out. I'll tell you frankly that this morning I was ready to do that. I still wish I had."

He smiled, but it wasn't much of a smile. "Anyway, I've called this meeting, and Dick Kassel here is working for the Club and with us and has established some facts. He's going to give us some advice and recommendations, and I know he'll welcome your questions. Dick?"

The lawyer looked at the five men sitting at the table. He was younger than any of them and was well aware they were men successful in their fields. He also respected them as men willing to help their Club. Such men, he knew, were individuals deserving of the highest respect. He talked straight, avoiding lawyer language.

"Gentlemen, what we have here is a situation unlike any I've ever experienced. My field is employment in the broad sense. But I also find myself involved in literally hundreds of different kinds of problems relating to that subject. I am deeply involved, as well, in dozens and dozens of sexual harassment cases. But this case, as you can imagine, goes far beyond sexual harassment. It's an item on a much larger agenda.

"It is obvious to me from my study of this matter, and without even knowing this man Phillips, that if he hadn't hooked on to the sex harassment issue, he would have found something else. This man's agenda is to manipulate the board and control the operation of the Club. His agenda obviously includes forcing all of you—and I mean not only the executive committee, but the entire board—out of office. He has made this a win-or-lose issue. He's shaking the dice for the entire pot.

"I remind you again that I do not know the man, but I feel right now that the course he has taken can lead to only one end. Two ends, I should say. First, if he wins, he will in effect be the untitled head of your Club. He will control policy, call most of the shots. He'll be a real hero to the membership, the guy who blew the whistle on the bad guys. If he loses, he will get kicked out of your Club. Obviously, based on what he's done, he thinks he'll win. You men have got some critical decisions to make, and you've got to make them tonight, I mean tonight, and then you've got to get moving with a specific plan.

49

"I've already determined that the two women involved deny any harassment. That's a very big positive thing! I doubt Phillips himself understands anything about the legal aspects of sexual harassment, but he undoubtedly has an attorney. Who his attorney is I have no idea. But I believe Phillips, from what you've told me, is too smart to undertake this battle without legal advice. I can't imagine any attorney, however, advising him to write the kind of letters he has written, so I think this was done on his own. I am also fairly well convinced that if Phillips has a smart attorney, that fellow knows the sexual harassment issue won't stand up. Maybe not. But I'm positive his attorney has not spoken to the two women as I have.

"You gentlemen know Mr. Phillips. I don't. And I am not looking forward to the day I first meet him. People like him are not my favorite members of society. Anyway, I am confident that we can win on the issue of sexual harassment. Now, another issue is his accusations and charges against Mr. Ashley and others, including Mr. Parsons here. Each of his charges is serious enough, God knows, but the charges against your manager, Claude Branch, are devastating in that they affect his employment not only now but in the future. As I see it now, and there may be lots I have yet to find out, Branch has a case against Phillips, a case he could easily win in court. I think, based on my experience in such things, that Branch could win a big number, at least a couple of million!"

The young attorney paused and looked around the room. There was not a sound.

"Phillips has exposed himself in several specific charges he has made against Mr. Manders. He has accused him of thievery. I have not talked to Mr. Manders, but I understand from Mr. Ashley that you have, Mr. Parsons?"

Parsons nodded. "Yes, I have. I am satisfied that the case is not thievery, but somewhat sloppy management, and even that not particularly serious. I did not, by the way, Mr. Kassel, talk to Mr. Manders about the charge of homosexuality. I refuse to get into that kind of thing."

"Good for you," said the lawyer. "Had you brought that up to Mr. Manders and done anything he could have interpreted as threatening his employment, he would have a case against you."

Parsons looked at the attorney, "Yes, I figured that, but over and above that, I know Manders pretty well. I have met his girlfriend. He plays on the Club's basketball team. He's a tough street kid. He's totally into sports. He's a guy. I mean a guy. And just so you know where I stand on the subject, if he were a homosexual, as long as he did his job and conducted himself properly, I'd be on his side."

Kassel again said, "Good for you. That's an enlightened point of view. All right, gentlemen, I'm going to make some recommendations. I've thought them through. From a legal standpoint, they are sound. Just as important, from the standpoint of proper procedure pertaining to Club matters, they are also sound.

"First, I recommend a letter from Charles Ashley, as president of the Club, to Mr. Phillips. The letter will acknowledge receipt of Phillips's letter and tell him he is violating specific Club policy as written in the bylaws. It will not be a legal-type letter, rather it is to be written in Mr. Ashley's style containing no threats, but firmly stating what Mr. Phillips cannot do, per the bylaws. Phillips probably will pay little attention to it, but it puts your Club on record. Further, it sets up a situation where, if it comes to that, you may come back at him later. And to put it bluntly, gentlemen, my reading of this situation tells me this will eventually come to your decision to dismiss Mr. Phillips from his Club membership. I have written a suggested letter for Mr. Ashley, in his style, which he has agreed to sign, and which I will read to you in a minute.

"Second, I urge each of you to keep your mouths shut about this matter. I am probably out of line to say that to such men as you, but this is a most serious matter and might well come to a court case. I want to be sure we are proceeding by the book."

He looked at each man. Each nodded in affirmation.

"Third, it is very important that none of you talk to Mr. Branch, Mr. Manders, Ms. Thompson, Ms. Esterbrook, or Gert Carlson about this. If it is necessary to talk to any of them on some other matter, by all means, do, but not about this. We have established that no sexual harassment took place, and Mr. Parsons feels no thievery has taken place. However, and please, Mr. Parsons, do not be offended by this, I am taking certain steps to satisfy myself as to the facts of the thievery business."

He looked at Parsons, who nodded.

Kassel continued, and Parson found himself feeling very good about this young lawyer and pleased that he was representing the Club in this very uncomfortable situation.

"Here is the letter I would like to go out over Mr. Ashley's signature:

Dear Mr. Phillips:

I have received my copy of the letter you have written and circulated to the membership of Pheasant Ridge. Your letter contained, among other things, several allegations about members of our staff and board of govenors.

This letter is to let you know that we are investigating each allegation. If it becomes necessary to conduct any investigation beyond what we have in mind, I assure you it will be done in a thorough and professional manner. My understanding is that you have already done your own investigation and have spoken with at least two Club employees in this regard. This is either true or not true, and if not true, I will expect you to set me straight.

I also understand you have obtained certain information in the form of chits and other paper records having to do with the personal obligations of specific Club members other than yourself. This is either true or not true, and if not true I expect you, once again, to set me straight.

I am told that you have personally approached and talked to our Club manager, Mr. Branch, and remonstrated him in a loud voice and in front of office staff.

This of course is against Club policy as stated in our by laws. If you had specific complaints as you have detailed in your letter to the membership, they should have been directed to the board, also as specified in the by laws.

As a longtime member of the Club, you are familiar, I assume, with the bylaws and why they are necessary to

51

ensure sound operation of the Club. If you have
not looked at the bylaws for some time, I urge you to do
so as soon as possible. The board is following the bylaws
in this matter, and we expect you to do so as well.

We ask that, starting immediately, you refrain from
contacting any employee for any reason other than
your own personal Club bill or any other strictly personal
matter. Your compliance to this request is very important.

Thank you.

The executive committee members, along with Parsons, agreed it was
a hell of a fine letter and should be sent immediately.

The letter was typed first thing the following morning and sent via certified mail to the home of Chester W. Phillips.

Phillips signed for the letter, then quickly carried it into his den and ripped it open. He read it through twice.

He told himself that Ashley had not written the letter. He then took the Club bylaws book from his desk drawer and read the pertinent section. He read the paragraphs again, and then mumbled to himself, Looks like those smart-asses are right. We'll see.

He sat down to his desk, took out a pen, and quickly wrote a note in longhand:

Dear Mr. Club President Ashley:

I have your note which was obviously not written by
you. The fact you are hiding behind the bylaws in this
matter tells me a lot. You certainly have a lawyer telling
you what to do. I guess I can understand because I doubt
any of the sleds on your so-called executive committee
could figure out what to say.

Don't feel too comfortable behind your bylaws
because I've just started on this thing, and I won't be
done until you've fired that manager of yours and
resigned yourself.

The note, typed by his secretary at the office, went out the next morning.

Six days went by and, except for the letter from Phillips the day after he'd received Ashley's note, there was nothing. Although some members of the board felt that maybe the problem was solving itself, Ashley knew that was not the case. Each day he winced as the phone rang and asked his secretary to bring the mail as soon as it came in.

Kassel called him on the seventh day, and when Ashley told him there was no response from Phillips, he allowed himself to think that just maybe the problem was going away. He was, of course, dead wrong.

On the eighth day, a letter arrived at Parsons's home. There was no return address. He did not have to open it to know where it came from.

To All the Pheasant Ridge Board:

Well, I see you've hired a hot-shot lawyer to come
after me. I know he wrote that letter I got from your
President Ashley. Fine, you want to play tough, I can play

tough.

You guys think you know best, and you hide behind the bylaws, so I know you have the guilty feeling. You are now telling me I have no business making suggestions in the best interests of the Club.We'll see about that. You can't hide, and you can't shut me up. In this letter I am demanding the immediate dismissal of Manager Claude Branch and the resignation of you, Mr. President. If both of these things are not done within twenty-four hours of the receipt of this letter, you are making one big mistake.

The Whistle Blower

Chapter Eighteen

The Complainers

Every golf club has them. They are a group of men who oppose just about everything their Club does. They sit together at lunch, always at the same table, usually several days a week. Their conversation centers around three basic items:

1. How much things cost today compared to years ago when they were younger.

2. Stupid decisions by the Club board and the way the Club is run.

3. The food served by the Club, the service, and the prices charged.

These men feed off each other. Each comment buys another, usually on the same subject, but stated in a louder voice. They are generally ill-informed but talk as though they are on the inside. They get their information via a mysterious grapevine. In order to enhance their own images, they frequently make things up, inventing scenarios that, as they develop them in conversation, seem to them to be the truth.

The group is not organized but seems to attract the same men day after day. They all seem to have money, they all seem successful in business, yet they may take a full two hours or more at lunch. At any given time, one or more of the group is just returning from a trip during which he played a minimum of four rounds of golf. In winter months, they return also from ski trips. Although they regularly eat lunch at the Club, no member of the restaurant staff remembers any one of them ever attending a social affair of the Club. Not one has ever been seen in the formal dining room with a wife. They do not serve on any of the Club's several committees. They come to the annual meetings, sit in one tight group and routinely oppose just about any plan for Club improvement.

These men are usually low-handicap golfers. They want the golf course to be immaculately maintained, yet they complain when the greens are being aerated on a Tuesday, one of their several golf days a week. If there is a plan afoot at the committee level for relocating a tee, they are against it. But they also complain, and loudly, that the golf course is never being improved.

They complain about slow play on the golf course, want far fewer members, with ladies' tee times restricted to the fewest number of hours a week. They like the golf professional, but think his line of merchandise is dismal and his prices too high.

They pay their dues, all the time voicing their discontent with the amount. In their wish for fewer members, it never occurs to them that their dues would be even higher if the membership were significantly reduced.

To the general good of the Club they contribute nothing.

On this particular day, there were six of them. Their conversation covered the basic three issues, but centered on the Chet Phillips's letters and his accusations.

"Did you hear what the board is going to do with Phillips? They are having a private dick follow him around."

"Where'd you hear that?"

"Friend of mine on the board told me."

"No shit? That's kind of dirty. I think Phillips is on to something."

"So do I. He's got all those facts, all those details. All that stuff about Ashley."

"I hear Ashley is ready to resign."

"I heard he's suing Phillips."

"Yeah, and so is Branch. I heard Phillips settled out of court."

"Really? How much?"

"Around a half million. And Branch must leave the Club."

"That's fine with me. He's a lousy manager anyway."

"As long as Branch is going, I wish he'd take Manders with him. The food's getting worse all the time."

"That's not Manders' fault, it's this guy Frank Parsons. I heard Parsons told Manders to cut the food budget by 20 percent."

"How can he do that?"

"Easy—he's in charge. He doesn't have to get approval from anybody."

"The prices are too high, anyway. A goddamn hamburger costs $4.50. I can remember when you could get a good hamburger for 50 cents."

"Hell, I can remember when I bought my house. It cost me less than it just cost me to fix up my kitchen."

"I just paid the tuition for my kid's first year at U Cal. Cost me more than I paid for four years in college."

"Yeah, I know that routine. My kid's car was four times what I paid for my Cadillac when I bought it."

"Did you hear the board hired a high-priced lawyer to defend the Club against Chet Phillips?"

"Yeah, I heard it was two lawyers. I know that law firm. They'll cost an arm and a leg."

"Why doesn't the board just all resign!"

"Yeah, that's what they should do."

"Did you hear what this guy Parsons said about the golf course? Said it didn't matter what kind of course we have. He wants to spend $10 million on the clubhouse."

"Parsons? Anybody know him? Does he play golf?"

"Yeah, he's a fifteen. What the hell does he care about the course?"

"That's what I want to know. How does a guy like that get to be chairman of the most important committee?"

"I heard he threatened Ashley with some kind of thing."

"Yeah, and Ashley should resign himself. Phillips has something there."

"I heard Ashley doesn't pay any dues. That's for being president."

"I can tell you for a fact the whole goddamn board is resigning."

"Best thing for the Club, that's for sure.

"Get a whole new group in there running the Club. Maybe then we could get better food for lower prices."

"Right. Did I tell you it cost me two grand just to get my front fender fixed at the shop? Two grand! I can remember when my first Cadillac cost less than that."

"Boy, ain't that the truth. My wife just had the bedroom done. Cost twice as much as I paid for the house."

"God, what's happening in this country?"

"Did you hear they're going to change the fourth green and add two traps?"

"No shit?"

"Did you hear Ashley and Phillips got into a fight?"

"Yeah, they're trying to hush it up."

"I was told they offered Phillips fifty grand to resign."

"Yeah, I heard that too. He told them to shove it."

"No shit?"

Chapter Nineteen

Committee Decision

In spite of the continuing problem with Phillips, the business of the Club had to go on. Parsons was now holding a committee meeting once a week, even when members could not attend. He had a personal timetable for completion of certain projects. The Club was now moving into the height of the season, with member participation at high level. It was an ideal time to be planning construction to start when the season began to slow down and eventually come to a halt with cold weather.

Frank's plan, which was quickly evolving based on thoughts of Ashley given to him months ago, was on schedule. He would at the next board meeting present his recommendations and ask for approval. The scope of the plan and its estimated cost did not call for membership approval. However, Parsons intended to present the plan to groups of interested members as soon as the board gave its approval.

The plan to this point called for only modest improvements but included making all restrooms handicapped accessible. His cost estimates told him the work required would cost less than $200 thousand. The Club had more than that in its capital improvements account. The money was available for just such work as was being considered. With these improvements under way during the fall, he and his committee would take a hard look at a long-range plan for upgrading the clubhouse from the ground up.

In a country club such as Pheasant Ridge, owned by the member shareholders, it would be necessary to get approval for major upgrading. Parsons planned to have his committee ready with such a plan for early fall presentation to the board and then the shareholders. He knew this would not be easy. There were, according to Ashley, at least two board members against any significant expenditures on the building. Both men knew the membership would be sharply divided on the upgrading issue. Parsons knew the process was likely to be unpleasant. But from long experience in consumer marketing and the steps needed for approval by a corporate client, he was not uncomfortable about any upcoming shareholder meeting. He had great confidence in the soundness of his thinking and his own ability to present it successfully.

In discussions with Ashley, whom Parsons kept informed on a week-to-week basis, both men were well aware that Phillips would be waiting to attack any ideas they might have. While it was not an entirely happy prospect, Parsons was actually anxious to take Phillips on head to head.

Parsons's committee had invited three interior designers to inspect the clubhouse and make presentations to the committee as to what they recommended. And, how much the work would eventually cost. Each designer presentation took one hour. Two of the designers were men, one a woman. After each designer was finished, Parsons thanked him or her and then asked his committee to comment.

"Well," said Laura Carter, "I surely wouldn't vote for that last guy, the tall one, whatever his name is!"

"Why is that, Laura?" another committee member asked, guessing the reason.

"Why? Well because he's obviously a homosexual, for God's sake! We don't need that. So it makes our choice much easier."

One of the women immediately took exception. "I don't care what he is if he has talent, and he obviously does, we ought to pick him."

Inwardly Parsons thanked her, and the discussion continued. Finally, although he did not really believe in running a committee in true democratic fashion, he suggested a vote. The tall homosexual (if indeed he was) got all votes but one.

Carter stood up, furious. "Well, I won't stand for this! And I'll tell you who won't either—most of the members and especially Chet Phillips!"

Parsons said evenly, "Laura, the vote was clear. That's the way it has to be. And any feeling that Chet Phillips might have is not going to influence this committee. While I might agree that some members may not like the idea of this fellow, I think most will agree it's the talent that really counts."

Carter glared at him. "I completely disagree, and if my feelings don't count for anything, then I'm off this committee!"

She walked quickly to the door of the meeting room. She turned and said, "You're all going to regret this, you're going to regret what you've done."

x x x x x x

"Chet, this is Laura Carter. Guess what the House Committee has just done? And that damn Frank Parsons. They've gone and hired a homosexual for the Club's design work. What do you think about that?"

"Laura," said Phillips, "We'll see about that. Thanks for telling me. This guy Parsons is gonna get a rude awakening."

Phillips turned to his yellow pad. On it he made four notations: "House committee. Queer. Parsons. Immediate action."

Chapter Twenty

The Response

Richard Kassel had written a letter to Phillips in response to Phillips's demands that Branch be fired and Ashley resign. Kassel, in no way intimidated by Phillips, deliberately waited a few days past the twenty-four hour deadline. (Kassel eliminated the normal salutation "dear" because he felt under the circumstances that the word was totally inappropriate.)

Mr. Phillips:

This letter is being written as a part of the ongoing communication between you and Pheasant Ridge Country Club. You should first understand that the board takes you very seriously. We have spent many hours on the issues you have raised. We have set aside, because of these issues, other matters the board considers very important. You should understand, therefore, that what you are doing is delaying action on subjects that have needed attention for some time.

As Mr. Ashley's previous letter informed you, the Club's bylaws specifically and clearly state that the kind of action you have taken is against Club policy. Let me repeat this—the actions you have taken to date are against the Club's written policy.

In our handling of these several matters, the board is following Club policy exactly. Recently you have once again taken an action that totally disregards policy.

You are in no position, Mr. Phillips, to demand that Manager Claude Branch be terminated. You are in no position to demand the resignation of President Ashley.

We believe further, that your demands are capricious, having as their objective the embarrassment of the board. We believe that your actions have as a second objective forcing the board to disregard Club policy, thus giving you the kind of leverage you appear, clearly, to be seeking.

You are hereby informed that the board will continue to follow policy. You are informed, further, that your recent demands will be ignored.

We ask now that you remove yourself from this matter and allow the board to pursue the matter to a reasonable conclusion. It is important that you

59

understand this.

You must disengage yourself from this matter. You must have no further contact with Club employees except as your actions are pertinent to your own account. You are informed that requesting information from Club employees, information having to do with the personal accounts of any member but yourself and your own family, is simply not permitted by the bylaws.

In a previous letter, you were asked to read these bylaws. Whether you have done so or not, I don't know. I do know, however, that any further action on your part that violates the bylaws will result in immediate response by the board.

When our investigation is complete, you will be informed. At that time, you will be given ample opportunity to respond to what we have determined to be the facts of the case. Until that time withdraw completely.

If you have any question as to the specifics and/or meaning of this letter, you would be well-advised to phone me at 311-7897.

Sincerely,

Richard W. Kassel

Chapter Twenty-one

Wheels Turning

At the same time Attorney Kassel was writing his letter to Phillips, Phillips was calling Marianne Esterbrook.

"This is your friend. You got anything more for me? I haven't heard from you lately."

"Sir, there is something going on here. I don't think I should be talking to you. I think I am being watched."

"What d'ya mean by that? Watched? Who's watching you for Christ's sake?"

"Well, I'm not sure `watched' is the right word. I feel that I am being, well, sort of looked at, and people are checking on me. And I might as well tell you I have been told I cannot give you any more information."

"Is that right? Who told you that? Who the hell told you that?"

"Please don't swear at me, sir. I can't tell you who. I can't tell you anything, I don't want you to call me any more."

"Dammit, Marianne, I'm not swearing at you. I'm just angry. They have no right to tell you you can't talk to me. All right, what about that stuff I asked you to get about Branch's expense report after his trip?"

"I've got that, sir."

"Well, send it to me. That happened before anyone told you to not give me any information. So it's okay."

"Well, sir, I'm not so sure. I'm very scared. I'm worried about my job."

"Marianne, may I remind you you've been paid for this information. Right? You've been paid.?"

Esterbrook realized that the man who had been so nice over a period of many weeks was now angry and talking to her as he would a servant.

"Yes, sir, you've sent me checks. Or you've had someone else do it. If you want the money back, you're welcome to it."

Phillips suddenly changed his tone, realizing he was close to losing the young woman as his informant.

"All right, Marianne. Wait. I'll tell you what. You send me that expense report stuff. That's okay because you got it before they told you not to give me any more stuff. It's okay, I promise you."

Close to tears, Esterbrook gave in. "Well, okay, sir. I'll mail it today. And if I get in trouble, you promised to help me, you know."

"I did," said Chet Phillips.

x x x x x x

Gomez, the chief engineer of the Club, was sitting in his apartment that night watching television and reading the paper. His phone rang.

"Bill, this is Mr. Phillips. I'm a member of Pheasant Ridge."

"Yes, I've heard of you, Mr. Phillips."

"Bill, I'd like to come and see you. Tonight."

"You want to come here? To my place? What's this about, Mr. Phillips?"

"I'll tell you when I get there, Bill. I'll be there in fifteen minutes."

"Wait, Mr. Phillips. My apartment is a mess. They're painting it. It's so bad my wife went to her mother's for a week until they're done. It's really a mess."

"That's okay, Bill, I'll be there soon."

"Wait a minute, Mr. Phillips, I'm not sure this is right. Why can you not tell me what it is you want to see me about?"

"All right, Bill. This is strictly confidential. Between you and me. I'm working on a secret project for the Club. It's most important I see you. You have no choice. You must talk with me. It's for the good of the Club. Do you understand this?"

Phillips knocked on the apartment door less than ten minutes later. He was not sure he would recognize Gomez, but when the man opened the door, he knew he had seen him often. Gomez was in working clothes, shirt open at the neck, and smoking a cigar.

"Mr. Phillips, I don't know what this is about. But I want to say this. I don't know anything about any secret project. I don't think I should be doing this. No one has said anything to me about it. I want you to know I am seeing you against my better judgement."

Phillips, not expecting this resistance, still moved into the room. There were painters' drop cloths everywhere. Gomez did not offer him a seat. Both men stood.

"Bill, as I told you, this is very important. I need information from you about this project we're working on."

Phillips's use of the word "we" gave Gomez a bit of comfort. It implied there were others involved. It must be okay, he thought. He pulled a drop cloth from one of the chairs and indicated Phillips could sit down.

"Okay, Bill, I'm going to ask you some questions, and I'll ask them one after the other. If you know the answer, just give it to me, and I'll go on to the next one. Shouldn't take long."

"Yes, sir." Gomez, still uncomfortable, watched Phillips carefully.

"First of all, how long have you been employed by the Club?"

"Ah, about twelve years, maybe nearer thirteen."

"And you're Mr. Branch's right-hand man as far as the clubhouse is concerned?"

"I don't know if I'm his right-hand man, sir. I'm the engineer."

"Okay, whatever. But you are with him a lot, right? And you are in lots of meetings?"

"Yeah, I guess so."

"Do you sit on house committee meetings?"

"Yes, sir, most of them."

"And you know Mr. Parsons?"

"Yes, sir." Gomez had increasing doubts about Phillips's objectives.

"Do you know about this interior decorator Parsons has hired?"

"I'm not sure what you mean by `know about' I was not aware Mr. Parsons had hired anyone."

"Are you saying you don't know the decorator is queer?"

Gomez was cool in his answer. "I am not saying anything about the decorator. I'm in no position to know anything about him. I know he made a presentation to the committee, and I know the committee discussed him and the other two decorators, too."

"But surely, Bill, you know the guy is a fag?"

"I know nothing of the kind, sir."

"But if he was a fag, would you want him in charge?"

"That's really none of my business, sir. First of all, the decorating of the Club is out of my line. Second, if the guy is good, I would think that would be the point. And third, I have great confidence in Mr. Parsons. He's a good man. He knows what he's doing."

"Okay, okay, Bill. Fine. Do you know what Parsons plans about the remodeling?"

"Only what I've heard in the meetings. Mostly, it's just making the restrooms handicapped accessible. A few other things. Nothing major. And then, after that is done, he will present a major upgrading plan to the board."

"How about to the members?"

"I know nothing about that, sir."

"Does Mr. Parsons sign chits for refreshments during your meetings?"

"I wouldn't know, sir. That's none of my business."

Phillips smiled one of his non-smile smiles. "Bill, you aren't being very cooperative. Surely, you know more than you are telling me. I have told you this is very important."

Gomez stood up. "Sir, I think this has gone far enough. I think you should leave. I will answer no more of your questions."

Phillips remained seated. "Mr. Gomez, this is an order. I order you to answer my questions. On behalf of the Club."

Gomez moved toward the door and opened it. "Mr. Phillips, no I will not. And Mr. Phillips, let me say this. I am a loyal Club employee. It seems to me you are looking for dirt. I won't participate in that. And also, I will report this conversation to my boss, Mr. Branch. And I imagine he will report it to the board."

Phillips stood up, furious. "You do that, and I'll sue your ass!"

x x x x x x

The next morning, Chet Phillips, an early riser, drove to the Club and walked quickly up to the office. He was sure no one would be there at that time, 7:15. The receptionist was not there, and the phone was being answered by voice message. There was a young man working in the far end of the space, and Phillips addressed him.

"Branch in yet? I guess not. What time does he usually get here?"

"Mr. Branch? Oh, he's usually here by eight or so."

"Eight or so? You mean he doesn't keep regular hours, he doesn't get here at the same time each day?"

The young man was instantly on his guard. "Yes, sir, he's very punctual. I'm sure he'll be here soon. Any minute."

Phillips stared at him. "What time does Mrs. Thompson get here?"

"She gets here early, sir, usually by this time, 7:30 or so."

Phillips said, "They'd better get here soon. This is a business office, not some damn country club." He did not realize what he had just said, and the young man was too nervous to react.

"What time does Ms. Esterbrook get here?"

The young man was now even more careful in his answer. He knew the member, whom he did not know, was not in the office for some, routine matter. He made his answer the fewest number of words possible.

"She's very punctual, sir."

Phillips snarled. "I didn't ask you about her habits, mister. I asked you when she gets here."

The man knew that here was a visitor looking for trouble. He remained quiet. Phillips walked back to the front of the office area.

"Okay, son, I'll be back to see you later. And I'll remember about your lack of cooperation."

At exactly 8 A.M. Branch walked in, immediately saw Phillips, and felt fear clutch at him. His hands became sweaty, and his stomach tightened. Before he could say anything, his secretary walked in and saw Phillips standing there, his legs wide apart, his face grim. She said nothing.

"Well," Phillips said, "I'm glad to see the office staff keeps some kind of hours. Where the hell is the receptionist? Why isn't she here? Isn't this a business office, for Christ's sake?"

Branch was now trembling, and Phillips, seeing it, pressed his advantage.

"It seems to me, folks, with all the problems we've got in this Club, people would get here early and get to work."

At that moment, the receptionist, a very young woman trainee, walked in and immediately looked scared.

Thompson knew that Phillips was here to prove something, and she had known for some time that Phillips was out to get her boss. She moved quickly to support Claude Branch.

"Mr. Phillips, we all get here at eight every morning. This is a very dedicated group of people. I don't know the problems you refer to, but I assure you we tend to business."

Phillips saw that she was a person with more backbone than he had expected, and he turned from her and looked directly at Branch. At that moment three more office employees walked in, followed by another.

"Yeah, I can see how dedicated everyone is. This is no way to run a railroad, Mr. Manager. We pay you a hundred grand a year. What do we get for it? We sure don't get promptness, and I'm sure we don't get much else either. Mr. Manager, your staff is to be here on time from now on, you got that?"

Branch was now soaked with sweat. "Yes, sir."

Phillips walked out of the office without another word.

Branch went into this office and sat down. He said nothing to his staff. Thompson took her pad and made some notes.

Phillips left the building and drove back to his office. The mail had just been placed on his desk. There were two envelopes he picked up immediately. One with no return address was from Marianne Esterbrook. The second carried the logo of the law firm of Richard Kassel. This one he opened first.

When he got to the end of the letter, he crumpled the paper in his fist and threw it across his office. He sat a moment, then got up, retrieved it, brought it back to his desk, and smoothed it out. He picked up his pen and began to write. He scribbled for several minutes, then called his secretary and told her to type the letter right away for his signature.

The secretary, knowing her boss, took the sheets of yellow paper and walked back to her desk. In her years of working for the man, she had become used to his style, his vendettas, his highs and lows. Nothing he did surprised her. She had often thought of leaving, but she was very well paid and the work was fairly easy. As she looked over what Phillips had written, she began to feel he had gone too far. One of the responsibilities she had assumed in her job was to occasionally protect her boss from himself.

She walked back into his office. "Mr. Phillips, it's really none of my business, and I probably shouldn't say this, but are you sure you want this letter written?"

Phillips looked up at her, amazed. "What the hell business is it of yours? Your job is to type what I write, not be a damn editor. Now I'm busy, and all I want you to do is what I tell you. I can get lots of secretaries to do that, you know."

She looked at him for a full thirty seconds, then turned and left, her lips trembling. She finished the letter and brought it in for his signature, saying nothing. Phillips read the letter, signed it, and went back to his work.

Dear Mr. Kassel:

I have your smart-ass letter. Now get something straight. No one tells me what to do, much less some smart-ass lawyer who gets paid twice what he's worth. I have uncovered some wrongdoing at the Club. I have found this out through careful investigation which has cost me money. But I am willing to sacrifice anything for the good of my Club. You don't investigate anything, you just do what your masters tell you to. You are dead wrong, and it will be found out.

You ask me to remove myself from this matter. No, that I will not do. I have a lawyer, too, you know, and he earns his money. If you were here right now, I would knock you on your lawyer ass. You are doing a cover-up and it won't be stood for.

Sincerely,

Chester W. Phillips
The Whistle Blower

After reading and responding to the attorney's letter, Phillips then turned to the letter he knew was from Esterbrook. She had provided him with information about the trip by the club manager made at the request of the Club president. The material was in considerable detail, and he spent the better part of an hour going over it. He covered his yellow pad with notes. He then picked up his phone and called his attorney.

"Fred, Chet Phillips. Well I got the goods on Branch now. I've got him right where I want him! So now we make our big move. I need to see you right away."

"Chet, let me say something. I'm your lawyer and what I do in your behalf is always in your best interests. I have to tell you this. I think you should stop. I think you should back off. You're getting in too deep. Stop and take a breath. It's for your own good."

"Wait a minute, Fred. Whose side you on, anyway?"

"I'm on your side, Chet. But you're out of line. You're out of control. I can see you painting yourself into a corner. Those guys on the board won't stand for much more of this. In fact, I'm betting they're up to here with you right now. They can kick you out of the Club, you know. It's within their right. Please, Chet. Knock it off. For your own good."

"Never! Never! I'll never back off. I'm in the right. They're wrong. They can't do anything, they haven't got the guts. And you better decide where you stand, Fred, or I'll find myself another lawyer. There are lots of them, you know."

"Chet! Listen to me. Listen very carefully. Don't ever threaten me. You want to get another lawyer, go ahead. Threatening me gets you nothing."

He hung up. He said to himself, Who the hell does that son of a bitch think he is?

Phillips, his face very red, said out loud, "That bastard, who the hell does he think he is?"

He left his office and drove to the Club. He put on his spikes and hit 100 balls on the practice range. He was going to have lunch in the grill but decided against it. He drove to the gas station, filled his tank, had the car washed, and then stopped at his bank. By the time he got back to his office, it was a little after 1 P.M.

His secretary had been seated at her desk, but she now got up and followed him into his office.

"Mr. Phillips, I have worked for you for more than four years. I believe I have done a good job for this company and for you. When I asked you if you really wanted to send that letter, I was serious. I was only doing what a good secretary should do, supporting and protecting her boss. I am the only member of my family with a good job. I need the money. But the way you talked to me when I said what I did was not fair. You said you could get lots of secretaries and you probably can. I am leaving. I will stay as long as it takes to train a new girl, that is, a new person."

Phillips's mouth curled in anger. "You don't need to stay a goddamn minute! Who needs you? Get out right now! Get out, get out. And don't take anything with you. No pencils, no pads, nothing!"

The woman stared at him in disbelief. "Mr. Phillips, you are even worse than I thought. I am not a thief. There's nothing here I could possibly want. You really are a terrible man."

Tears began to stream down her face. She drew herself up, took a deep breath, walked to her desk, took out a few personal items and left the office area. As she stood waiting for the elevator, she began to cry very hard.

As she stepped into the elevator, Phillips came storming into the lobby area. He shouted at her, "And don't say anything about this to anybody, you understand? You do and I'll sue your ass!"

The elevator doors closed.

Chapter Twenty-two

The Motion

Chuck Ashley called a special session of his board, and rather than do it at the clubhouse, he reserved a private room at a local restaurant. They would not be disturbed. In selecting the place, his instinct told him it was entirely possible Phillips would walk into the meeting if he knew where it was to be held. In scheduling the meeting, Ashley cautioned each board member to keep the place of the meeting confidential.

He called the meeting to order. All but two members were present. "Guys, this Phillips thing is out of control. I've never been so mad in my life. The problem, instead of going away, is ever worse. I'm a tough son of a bitch, but I don't know how much more I can take.

At this point, the phone in the restaurant room rang and was answered by Ashley, who listened for a few seconds, then hung up. He turned to the board. "That was the Club office, the after-hours receptionist. There's a fax at the office, addressed to all of us. It will be delivered to us here. I don't know what it says. I think we can all figure out who sent it. Anyway, let's start the meeting, and when it gets here we'll deal with it."

Ashley then turned over the meeting to Richard Kassel. As Kassel started talking, Parsons again found himself thinking well of the way Kassel handled himself: cool, sure, no-nonsense. He again told himself the Club was lucky to have such a man on their side.

Kassel said, "Gentlemen, I've told you previously I have never encountered such a situation in my professional life. It's beyond anything in my experience. We have determined to our complete satisfaction there was no sexual harassment. None. We have determined there are at least two moles on the Club staff who have furnished Mr. Phillips with information. We have told these people they must stop. We have told Phillips to stop talking to them and to restrict his requests for information to his own Club accounts. Phillips is paying no attention to us. He is not satisfied. He is determined to keep this issue alive, not only in his attacks on Mr. Ashley with respect to Mr. Ashley's account, but has made other accusations, some of which you know about.

"I will say, at this point, that you may wish to get another attorney to handle the situation as it has developed. My expertise is in employee relations, and this case is going well beyond that. If you choose to hire another attorney, I will understand. That is your call."

Ashley looked around the room. "Dick, we feel you are our man. We want you to continue." He looked at his board for affirmation. Heads nodded.

Kassel continued. "Thank you, gentlemen. Although I am not sure that I will be thanking you some time in the future. I fully expect this entire matter to be ugly, that some of us might get hurt, and that no matter how it ends, the Club itself is going to take some severe hits.

"I don't know what this fax is going to say, but I'm as sure as you all seem to be that it is from Mr. Phillips. My gut tells me it will contain some new allegations and threats. So let me tell you where things stand and what I recommend.

"First, Phillips will continue his attacks, and we will have to react.

Phillips has flatly refused—in a near hysterical letter to me—to stop his attack, to disengage himself, and to refrain from further employee contacts. He has at least two information sources and probably more than that.

Knowing the man as I do now, I fully expect him to sue the Club. He has no real grounds for a suit, but he can cause all of us a lot of problems, and it can cost the Club a lot of money. Phillips has been quoted as having a lot of money he is willing to spend on this matter.

There is a lot more I could say, but I think it's time to take some positive action on the matter and not be continually on the receiving end."

As various board members reacted positively to that statement, there was a knock at the door of the room, and Ashley walked over and opened it. A young Club employee handed him an envelope. Ashley opened it and read the contents. There appeared to be but one sheet of paper. His face nearly white, Chuck Ashley read the note aloud:

To the board of Pheasant Ridge Country Club:

For some time, I have been pointing out to you the poor performance of our Club management, and several staff people, and certain members of the executive committee and board.

I have questioned the ethics of your president, Mr. Ashley. Although I have done this repeatedly, nothing has been done. All you have done is hire a smart-ass lawyer who sends me fancy letters.

I know you are having a special meeting tonight, away from the Club to hide from me. Never mind that kind of smart-ass stuff. I have ways of finding out anything.

In view of all this, I hereby demand that in your meeting tonight you terminate Mr. Claude Branch without any more delay. I demand that your President Ashley resign tonight. I demand that restaurant Manager Russell Manders be terminated tonight. Further, I demand that board members Costello and Parsons remove themselves from the board tonight.

If these actions are not taken in your meeting tonight, I intend to sue the Club on the basis of what I have previously brought up. I am accusing several people of gross mismanagement, theft, and highly improper behavior.

I am dead serious, gentlemen. I have set aside a large amount of my own money to pursue this thing to a satisfactory ending.

Chester W. Phillips,
The Whistle Blower.

One board member, not raising his hand, said, "Where did the son of a bitch find out we were having a meeting tonight? What the hell is going on? Who is giving him this stuff?

Other board members reacted in kind. Kassel said nothing. Ashley struggled to get control of himself. Frank Parsons was formulating a motion he would make when the group finally gathered itself.

While the group was reacting to the fax from Phillips, Kassel was thinking through what he would now recommend. He had pretty well decided what the plan should be, but Phillips's remarks in the fax would cause some alteration in strategy and tactics. He waited, relaxed, for Ashley to bring the group back to order.

After perhaps three minutes, Chuck Ashley clapped his hands for attention. "All right, guys, let's come to order. Anyone may speak. I'll recognize you in turn. Yes, Frank?"

Parsons said, "Thank you, Mr. President. From the beginning of this affair, I've been shocked and angered that a member of this Club could do something like this. I have never liked Chet Phillips, but I have acted courteously toward him—with perhaps one exception. I'm a new member of this board but a longtime member of the Club, as you all know. I think we have been screwing around long enough, no offense to you, Chuck, but I think it's time to act. I think we must kick this guy out of the Club. We have reason to do so, God knows."

Several members immediately stated their agreement. Ashley said, "Will you put that in the form of a motion, Frank?"

"Absolutely. I move we start immediately the proceeding which has as its objective the removal of Chester Phillips from membership in Pheasant Ridge."

There were immediate seconds from three different men.

Larry Costello raised his hand and Ashley recognized him.

"Frank, I agree with you as obviously most of us do. But as an attorney, and with my attorney's eye on the bylaws, we can't do what you are recommending. At least, not in that sense."

Costello looked at Kassel, who nodded without speaking.

Costello, looking at Parsons said "Much as I want to kick this guy's ass out of the Club, there is a procedure and we must follow it. Only a handful of members have ever been expelled, and it's got to be by the book. Obviously, it's a very serious matter. We simply can't move on a motion that states we are going to expel a guy. If we decide to initiate the procedure, it would have to be to call a hearing and give Mr. Phillips a chance to respond to any charges we would make. If, following that hearing, we then decide to take certain action, that is the way to do it. I admit, Frank, it's maybe the same thing in the end, but it's got to be by the book."

Parsons nodded. "I understand. I withdraw my motion as stated. I move, instead, that we follow the procedure, as called for in the bylaws, leading to a hearing for Mr. Phillips at a time and date when all or most board members can attend."

Costello nodded his approval. "Do I have a second?" said Ashley.

Ten members shouted in unison, "Second!"

Chapter Twenty-three

Letters and Action

Kassel grinned. "I think I get the sense of the board's feelings. All right, let me tell you what now must be done. First, we must permit Mr. Phillips to appear before this board at the earliest mutually agreeable date and time. He will be allowed to present his case formally, with no time restrictions. Two, we must provide at that meeting a non-involved person, a recorder, if you please. Someone who will take detailed notes of the meeting of what is said and by whom. Third, there must be a quorum of the board. Fourth, and difficult as this may be, we must be prepared to listen to Mr. Phillips with all due respect, and under no circumstances should we allow Mr. Phillips to get the impression this is some kind of kangaroo court."

His eyes surveyed the room. He saw heads nodding.

"Okay, if it is the board's agreement that these steps should be put in position and followed, I will so inform Mr. Phillips by mail tomorrow. May I get a feeling from you members as to when this hearing should take place? Let's see if we can find the best possible date from the standpoint of attendance."

After a small amount of discussion and comments by individual members as to their near future travel plans, a date was set. Kassel asked for an alternative date, and that too was agreed upon. It appeared that all but three of the board could attend either date selected.

"All right, gentlemen, I will draft the letter to Mr. Phillips immediately. It will be sent certified mail."

Certified letter from Richard Kassel to Chester Phillips:

> In response to your charges against various persons on the staff and board of governors, you are hereby invited to present your charges and accusation at a special meeting of the board at 5:30 P.M. on June 30.
>
> All provisions of the Club's bylaws will be strictly enforced at this meeting. The board will be instructed to follow carefully all the rules stated in the bylaws. You, as well, will be expected to follow all the rules.
>
> A non-involved recorder will be present throughout the entire meeting. You will have adequate time to present your case, but we suggest you try to keep it within an hour. If this is not possible, please try to put some limit on it yourself. This is only in the interest of yourself and all board members so that everyone can get home at

a reasonable time.

You have made some serious charges, and the board will expect specific evidence to support those charges. I urge you not to use innuendo nor to use statements that are not backed up by pertinent facts, figures, or other means.

There will be a chairman running this meeting. He is a board member, Mr. Gordon Knowles. I believe Mr. Knowles is well- known to you and unless I hear to the contrary, we will assume Mr. Knowles is acceptable to you.

I would point out to you at this time that it is not necessary for us to get your approval of the meeting chairman (see bylaw #14-C) but we are extending this courtesy to you. The meeting will be held in the Club board room.

Please verify to me your acceptance of this date and time and your acceptance of Mr. Knowles via my direct office phone as listed on the letterhead. I ask that you also write me a letter specifying your acceptance.

Sincerely,

Richard Kassel

Certified letter from Chester Phillips to Richard Kassel:

Dear Mr. Kassel:

I have your recent letter asking me to attend a meeting of the Pheasant Ridge Board on June 30 at 5:30 P.M. Although I have another meeting scheduled at that time, I will cancel said meeting. I do not, however, accept your specification of a "non-involved" recorder, whatever that is. I demand a licensed court reporter, and unless one is provided, I will not attend the meeting because under those circumstances, it would be a rigged meeting.

Sincerely,

Chester Phillips
The Whistle Blower

Certified letter from Richard Kassel to Chester Phillips:

Dear Mr. Phillips:

I have your letter which first appears to accept our invitation. However, you later state you will not be present unless—and you "demand" this—a licensed court reporter is present.

For your information, the bylaws specifically state that for such a meeting, a non-involved recorder will be present and that such a person will be there at Club expense. Your "demand" is inappropriate.

If you refuse to attend this hearing based on this issue, we have no choice but to assume you are passing on making formal charges. If this is the case, the board will then be obligated to move ahead with the procedure according to the Club bylaws in such cases.

Sincerely,

Richard Kassel

Certified letter from Chester Phillips to Richard Kassel:

Dear Mr. Kassel:

It appears I have no choice but to accept your terms for a rigged meeting. I will be there, and your rubber stamp board better be ready with their t's crossed and i's dotted.

Sincerely,

Chester Phillips
The Whistle Blower

Letter from Charles Ashley to board members:

We now have confirmed through our attorney, Dick Kassel, that Mr. Phillips has accepted our invitation to a hearing. At this meeting he will make his formal charges. The meeting is set for June 30 at 5:30 P.M. in the Governor's Room.

Mr. Phillips will have one hour, more if he needs it, to make his presentation. There will be a non-involved recorder present to take notes on the proceedings.

It is important you be there, and that you give Mr. Phillips your full attention with no interruptions.

I need hardly remind you that this meeting is to be held in the strictest confidence. Thank you for your support and patience in this matter.

Sincerely,

Charles Ashley

On receipt of the second Kassel letter, Phillips called his attorney, Fred Webber. The two had not spoken since the phone call weeks earlier that had ended in anger.

"Fred, I've accepted the Club's invitation to appear at their hearing. It's June 30. I've insisted on a court reporter being present, but they're stonewalling me. Can you be there with me?"

"Chet, that would be inappropriate. I'm sure this hearing does not call for attorneys. And even if it did, I think my presence would be viewed in a negative way by the board. And if they say they won't provide a court reporter you can bet they've checked on that. Among other things a court reporter would cost them a lot of money, and I'm sure at this point, they feel this mess has cost them too much as it is. Sorry, Chet, but I can't be there that night."

"Christ, Fred, you can't desert me!"

"Chet, be reasonable. I'm not deserting you, although after your last phone call, I'd have every reason to. This meeting is not one where an attorney is an appropriate participant. You should go to that meeting with the objective of settling this thing, not attacking any further. That's good advice, and I urge you to follow it."

"So you're leaving me out on a limb, huh?"

"Oh, Chet, for Christ's sake, knock it off. That crap doesn't work with me and you know it!"

"Fred, I only know I'm counting on you and you're letting me down. Maybe I should think about getting me another lawyer."

"Chet, that's enough! You want another lawyer, get one. No lawyer I know could get you out of the mess you've got yourself into. It's a lost cause. This hearing is your golden chance to wiggle out of this without getting kicked out of the Club. That's all I've got to say to you. Good luck."

Webber hung up.

Chapter Twenty-four

The Hearing

At 5:25 on the evening of June 30, Chet Phillips opened the door to the governor's room and walked in. There was a smirk on his face as if to let the board members know he was not scared. His eyes quickly ran over the faces of the men sitting around the table. Only one member of the board was missing.

At 5:30 Ashley said, "Mr. Secretary, do we have a quorum?"

"Yes, Mr. President."

To this point Ashley had not acknowledged Phillips, and only one or two of the board had nodded to the man.

"I declare this is an official meeting of the board of governors of Pheasant Ridge Country Club. This meeting is a hearing. There will be no other business conducted. Mr. Chester Phillips, a shareholder of the Club, will make a presentation of his charges as he has earlier brought up. The meeting will be conducted strictly by the rules of the bylaws. Mr. Phillips will have one hour—more if he needs it—to make his presentation. There is a non-involved recorder present to take detailed notes. This too is as specified by the bylaws. I ask our board members to listen to Mr. Phillips without interruption. Mr. Phillips, questions from various board members will be permitted following your presentation. Are you ready to begin?"

Phillips, the smirk still on his face, looked directly at Ashley. "Mr. President, I'm interested to know just what a `non involved' recorder is?"

Ashley was dead serious in his response. "A `non-involved' recorder, as specified by our bylaws is first, a person who can take shorthand or who has a recording device; second, `non- involved' means this person is not a member of the Club nor someone who is familiar with the workings of the Club. Today this person is Mr. Ferris Hutton, who qualifies on both points. Mr. Hutton is a certified public accountant by trade and has served as a recorder on several occasions. He is not known to anyone on our board and was recommended to us. After the hearing he will provide us with a written report. This report will be available on request from anyone in this room. Anyone."

The smile remained on Phillips's face. "Well, I guess I'll have to be satisfied with that. At this point I ask the `recorder' to make note that I had requested a court reporter at this meeting."

He stared at Ferris Hutton, who nodded.

The room was totally silent, members looking straight at Phillips.

Phillips got up. "All right, I'll begin."

Parsons, looking at the man, saw that rather than have a business-like method of presentation, such as the use of an overhead projector, Phillips simply had a handful of yellow sheets. From where Frank sat, he noted that the material was all handwritten. As a man who had made literally hundreds of presentations as a part of his consulting and marketing work, Parsons was dismayed.

Phillips began by making several ad lib remarks. "Well, not having the resources this board does, with your attorneys and your access to presentation facilities, I'm just going to have to get along the best I can. I'm just going to read my comments."

No one said anything. The room was deadly still.

Phillips then started to read from the first page. He continued for a minute or so, then said that he was having trouble reading his own notes. It became clear within a few minutes that what he was presenting was largely a repeat of his earlier charges with more detail. He moved from point to point loosely, his voice occasionally emotional. From the beginning to about the middle, he had very little presence, and he seemed to realize he was not being effective. Parsons wondered how this man, so successful in business, had survived while being a very ineffectual communicator.

When Phillips had been on his feet talking continuously for about fifty-five minutes, Parsons saw that he had worked his way through no more than half the yellow sheets. Phillips noted Ashley glancing at his watch.

"How my doing?" he asked, still with the humorless smile.

"You have something around five minutes left, Mr. Phillips."

"Are you going to hold me to that?"

"No, sir, we have told you that you could have additional time if needed."

Phillips looked in the direction of the recorder. "Make note of the fact I am being pressured to finish."

Ashley started to respond, then kept silent.

Phillips speeded up but still proceeded shakily. He reached his last page twenty minutes later. The flat looks on the faces in front of him told him he had done a poor job.

He spread his legs apart in a more confrontational stance and stuck his chin out. "Well, I'm through. All I've got left to say is if you guys don't start doing things right, if you don't get rid of some of the bad apples around this Club, you're gonna bring this Club to its knees. Did you get that, Mr. Recorder?"

Ferris Hutton nodded.

Ashley sat quietly, then asked if there were questions from the board members. No one spoke. Finally one member raised his hand. "It's possible I misunderstood what was going to happen in this meeting, Mr. President? It was my take that we were going to hear or see proof of the accusations that have been made. I have heard no proof. All I have heard is a restatement of the original charges plus a few new ones. I heard again about the sexual harassment charges. I thought we had established some time ago that there was no sexual harassment."

Phillips glared at the man. "If a boss puts his hands on his secretary's neck, that's sexual harassment in my book."

The member looked right back at him. "Well, your book is not what we're operating on. Proof is proof. Neither of the two women you have spoken of has claimed sexual harassment. Further, maybe I missed something, but I heard no proof that anyone stole anything from the kitchen. We've been sitting here for an hour and a half and as far as I'm concerned, we're no further along than we were when we walked in here!"

Phillips looked at Ashley. "This is just what I thought. This is all rigged against me. It's a kangaroo court. Did you get that, Mr. Recorder?"

Ferris Hutton nodded again.

Ashley, still outwardly calm, looked around the room. "Any other questions or comments?"

No one spoke.

Larry Costello raised his hand. "Mr. Phillips, as you know, I am an attorney, and as an attorney I'm trying to be as objective as possible. In that regard my question to you is do you feel this hearing has been conducted by the rules of the bylaws and therefore impartial in its treatment of you?"

Again the mirthless smile appeared on Phillips' face. "I don't know. There's the business of the absence of a court reporter, which I had demanded. And there's this comment just now."

Costello persisted. "You have made a considerable point about the reporter. I cannot see how it is pertinent who takes the notes as long as the person is competent. My question still is do you feel this hearing has been impartial and fair?"

Phillips said, "I don't know. Maybe."

Costello persisted, "That really doesn't answer my question. Do you feel you have been treated impartially here tonight?"

"Yeah, I suppose so."

"Is that a `yes'?"

"Yes, that's a `yes', answered Phillips, neatly painted into a corner by the Club secretary.

Costello could not resist the temptation of his response.

Looking at the recorder, he said "Did you get that, Mr. Recorder?"

Ferris Hutton nodded.

The members of the board, amused by Costello's final remarks, now began to file out of the room. Phillips was among them. Before anyone got to the door, it burst open and Restaurant Manager Russell Manders came into the room. He was a big man, 6' 2", and as he stood just inside the door, he put his hands on his hips and stared directly at Phillips.

"All right, I want to talk to the guy who's been telling lies about me!"

x x x x x x

Following Manders's almost shocking confrontation of Phillips, Ashley had grabbed Manders by the elbow, spoken quietly to him, and slowly walked him out of the room ahead of the rest. Before Phillips reached the door, Ashley had Manders whisked out of the area and down the stairs.

Most of the members were relieved, but one said in a loud enough voice for Phillips to hear, "Too bad, Russ would have flattened Chet, and it would have been good enough for him!"

Phillips turned to see who had made the remark. He made a mental note not to forget.

x x x x x x

As Phillips left the Club, he drove to his office rather than home. Most everyone had left for the day, and he went to his office, turned on the lights, and sat down to his desk. He was there better than an hour, writing as fast as he could.

76

Shortly before noon on the Saturday following the hearing, Parsons heard the sound of mail being pushed into his box. As he walked to pick it up, he felt a strange sensation, and the hair on the back of his neck tingled. He knew something special was going to be in that box along with the usual bills, flyers, and personal letters. He was right. There was the envelope with the words printed on the face:

"IMPORTANT BIG NEWS FOR PHEASANT RIDGE MEMBERS!"

As he looked at the envelope, there was a tightness in his stomach, and he thought about putting the envelope aside. He had planned to have lunch at the Club and play with his usual foursome. He did not want the certain unpleasantness of yet another Phillips' letter on his mind as he teed off. But he simply could not put the envelope aside. He ripped it open.

TO ALL DUES-PAYING SHAREHOLDERS OF PHEASANT RIDGE

Here is the very latest on what the rulers of our Club are pulling on you, the innocent, non-elected members. Here is what is being done to tear down the proud tradition of the finest golf and country Club in America. What is going on will sicken you.

First, let me tell you about something that has just happened. The other night I was invited to appear before the board of governors. The purpose, as I was told, was to give me a chance to make formal charges against certain individuals. I was told I would have unlimited time, time that was needed to properly communicate the many wrongdoings by staff and officers of the Club. Instead I was cut off at about an hour and given only a few moments to finish, so I was not able to say everything I had wanted to say.

In addition, prior to the meeting I had demanded that a professional court reporter be present. When I got there, however, I quickly perceived that there was an amateur there taking notes.

Attached to this letter is proof of all the charges I have made, and you will see that I have been speaking the noble truth. But let me quickly tell you this. First, although our board now denies it ever happened, your manager, Mr. Claude Branch, is guilty of sexual harassment. They have whitewashed this serious matter, and while they have managed through serious intimidation to get the women to change their stories, I have a witness.

Further, I now have proof that Mr. Branch, while on Club business in Cleveland, cheated on his expense account and also spent considerable time with a female who is not his wife, and made many phone calls to her, all paid for by the Club, and two dinners, also paid for by the Club. What these two cuties were doing and talking about is anybody's guess. Incidentally, Mr. Branch still has not written a report of what he was supposed to be doing on this Club-paid-for business.

There's lots more (see enclosed records and proof). One final thing, however. As I was leaving the room after the kangaroo court, excuse me, "hearing", I was accosted by Mr. Russell Manders, our esteemed restaurant manager. He is a very big man, and I was physically threatened.

See next pages. I have vowed to stay at this investigation and see it to the end, no matter the cost to me. And no matter how many fancy lawyers (paid for by your dues) threaten me.

I am spending my own money for all this work and investigation; nobody is giving me anything.

Are you proud of the way your Club is being run by these scum of the earth officers and employees? If not join with me in my holy crusade.

Sincerely,

Chester W. Phillips
The Whistle Blower

In addition to the several hundred Pheasant Ridge shareholders who got copies of this letter were the presidents of all the many golf clubs in the area. Also receiving a copy was Mrs. Claude Branch.

Chapter Twenty-five

The Complainers

At the round table in the corner of the Club grill two days later, the group was concentrating on Phillips's latest letter.

"Geez, did you read that? He called them `scum of the earth.'"

"Yeah, I read it, and I think he went a little too far. He's just askin' to be kicked out."

"Ah, they can't kick him out. He's been around too long. Besides, he's got proof. Can't kick him out if he's got proof."

"I know for sure he's got more on them than he's written about. I know for sure that this guy Parsons is gettin' a kickback from the decorating studio. I hear it's five grand!"

"Really? I hadn't heard that. But I do know that Chuck Ashley not only doesn't pay dues, but he gets his guests on the course for nothing. How about that?"

"Did you hear Manders decked Chet? Right there in the board room! Knocked him out. I mean unconscious."

"No shit?"

"No shit. Two board members told me that."

"Yeah, I heard Manders knocked him down, then picked him up and knocked him down again. Coulda killed him. Manders is a big dude."

"But Manders is supposed to be a queer."

"Yeah, one board member told me they know for sure that Manders lives with a guy."

"Well, anyway, looks like we'll have a new Club president."

"How d'ya know that?"

"Friend of mine on the board told me so. Said Ashley resigned that same night."

"No shit?"

"I've got one for you. The estimate for the remodeling came in, and it was a half million over the original. But the committee is going ahead anyway."

"No shit?"

"No shit."

"Didja hear that Phillips is gonna sue Larry Costello?"

"Honest to God, for how much?"

"I heard a million."

"No shit?"

x x x x x x

The phone rang in Frank Parson's office. "Have you read that letter?"

79

It was Ashley.

"Yes, I have. He's not only sick, he's stupid."

"Anyway, Frank, I'm calling a special meeting of the board for next Tuesday. Can you make it?"

"Count on me, Chuck."

"Good. I knew I could."

Richard Kassel's phone had rung several times starting first thing in the morning. There were four calls from board members. "Dick, this is Chuck Ashley. You probably have heard. Phillips has written another letter. We can't screw around any more, Dick. I want you to start whatever it is you have to do to have a meeting for expulsion."

x x x x x x

Larry Costello called Ashley. "Chuck, I just got a call from a friend of mine at National Golf Club. He's on their board. Their Club president got a copy of the letter from Phillips. And he had had a call from the president of Green Trees Club. He'd got the same letter too, for God's sake!"

"Well," said Ashley, "our move is clear now. I've just spoken with Dick Kassel. Told him to get ready for an expulsion proceeding. See you Tuesday night. We'll find out from Kassel just what to do next."

x x x x x x

Ashley's phone rang once more. "Mr. Ashley, you don't know me, but I'm Leonard Clement. I'm the mayor of Bridgeside. I think you should know that I just got a letter, rather, a copy of a letter that one of your members has sent to me. Man named Phillips. You know him?"

"Yes, I know him."

"Well, I knew you'd want to know. Two of your Pheasant Ridge members are on my city council being as your Club is within our city limits. Anything you want me to do about it?"

"No, thank you, Mr. Clement. This fellow is causing us lots of trouble. I appreciate your letting me know."

"You're welcome. Sounds like trouble. If it is, good luck."

x x x x x x

As Phillips got home in the early evening, his phone was ringing. He walked quickly to it.

"Dad, this is Cory. I need to talk to you."

"Cory, I just got home, and I've got a lot of work to do. Can this wait?"

"No, I don't think so. I really need to talk to you. I'd like to come over right now. This is important."

At 6:30 P.M. Phillips heard a key turning in the lock on the back door of his home, and he walked to greet his youngest son. They had never been close. In Chet Phillips's eyes, Cory was a rebel, a long-hair, and very liberal politically. He had no idea what Cory wanted to talk about, but he led the young man into his living room and motioned for him to sit down.

"Okay, Cory, what's up? Are you in trouble again?"

"No, Dad, I'm not. But you are. This isn't about me, it's about you."

"Cory, let's stop screwing around and get to it. What the hell is it?"

"Dad, it's about you and this business with the Club. About what you're doing. About all these damn letters you're writing. You're making all kinds of accusations against some pretty neat guys. Everybody's talking about it. I think you should stop."

"Stop? You want me to stop? You got any idea what you're talking about, Cory?"

"Yes, I think I have got an idea. I think you're wrong. My friends think you're nuts. I'm sorry to say that, but it's true. Most of the members are against you."

"Most of the members? How do you know that? You done a survey or something? What are you, George Gallup or something?"

"Dad, please don't talk like that. Please listen to me. What you're doing is wrong. No, I haven't done any survey for God's sake, but lots of people are saying you should stop. I hear things. I get these phone calls from guys. At first some of the members thought you were on to something. Now they just think you're on some kind of vendetta."

"Cory, you're messing around in something you don't know anything about. This is none of your damn business. I know what I'm doing, and I don't have to justify anything to you. The Club is being run by a bunch of crooks and queers, and I'm not gonna let them get away with it. Now if that's all you came for, forget it. Get the hell out. You're out of your league."

"Dad, I thought that's what you might say. It's the way you've always talked to me when I try to tell you something. What I'm saying is for your own good. You're ruining yourself at that Club. They'll kick you out, don't you see that? Why can't you see that?"

"What I can see is something you'll never see, Cory. You're just like your mother, no sense of reality. That's why you've never been able to hold a job, why you'll never get anywhere in real life. And if this is all you wanted to talk about, there's no sense in continuing this conversation."

He got up and moved toward the back door of the house. His son looked at him, knowing this was what he had expected, but miserable that he had not been able to get through. And worried that his father was heading toward some kind of wreck.

He said, "Okay, Dad, I'll go. I can see I'm not getting anywhere. But I'll make one last plea for you to stop. Why do you always have to control everything? Why can't you just once back off something?"

"Cory, that's it. I've got work to do. Good night."

"All right, Dad. I've tried. Like I always try. Sometimes you're right and sometimes you're wrong. This time, you're dead wrong. And I know you're going to end up sorry."

"What the hell do you mean by that? What the hell are you talking about, Cory?"

"Dad, they're going to kick you out of the Club!"

"Like hell they are! They haven't got the guts. There'd be a revolution out there if they tried. They'd all be thrown out on their ass."

"Well, Dad, I think you're overestimating your popularity.
Anyway, I'm resigning from Pheasant Ridge. I can't live with what you're doing."

"You're resigning? Hell, you're just a junior member, that's all, just a damn junior member. You can't even vote! Who the hell cares whether you resign, anyway?"

The young man opened the back door, and without another word left the house. He got into his car in the driveway and pulled away.

x x x x x x

Phillips walked quickly to his phone. He punched out the numbers and waited for the ring at the other end.

"Fred, this is Chet."

The attorney, instantly alert, knew Phillips was not calling him at home in the evening for idle chatter.

"Chet, I'm not your damn attorney any more, remember?"

"Oh, the hell with that. Of course you're my attorney. You can't just drop me, you know. You know too much about me and the business."

"Chet, oh yes I can. And anything I know is between us, for God's sake. What the hell kind of man are you, anyway?"

"Fred, let's stop screwing around here. I want you to take Cory out of my will. Right now. Tonight."

"You want Cory out of your will? What the hell is it, Chet? What's going on with you? Have you thought about this?"

"Yeah, I've thought about it. Do it. And send me a copy when it's done"

"Chet, listen to me. All right, I'll do it. But get this. This is my last act in your behalf. After this, I'm through, you got that?"

"I got it. Screw you, Fred." He hung up.

x x x x x x

The next day, just before noon, Parsons went to the Club for what he hoped would be a short meeting with Branch. There were still some unanswered questions having to do with the construction. He had found Branch to be very helpful in such meetings, knowledgeable, and with good judgement as to how members would react to certain ideas.

As Frank walked into the restaurant area, he saw that Phillips was sitting at the first table inside the room.

Phillips looked up. "Just the guy I want to see. I've been sitting here twenty-six minutes and I still don't have my soup!"

Parsons knew the question was being addressed to him because as House Committee chair, all restaurant activity came under his overall responsibility. Still, he asked the question, "Why are you telling me about it?"

"Why I thought you were the big cheese in this restaurant, isn't that right?"

"I'm no big cheese, and I don't know why you've been waiting for twenty-six minutes. Let's get Russ Manders out here and find out."

It was quickly apparent that Phillips wanted no part of the restaurant chief.

"I think this is something the House Committee chair should know about."

"Okay, Mr. Phillips, I'll go find out." Parsons walked back into the kitchen area where Manders was talking to a waiter.

"Russ, what's the story on Phillips waiting twenty-six minutes for his soup?"

Manders, who respected Parsons, let his face reflect his anger.

"Jesus, sir, did he say something to you? Sure, he did. Let me tell you what happened. First we got him his bowl of soup within minutes of his order. He said it was not what he had ordered. He said he'd ordered bean and what we brought him was cream of celery. So Ellie here brought him bean, and he tried it and said it was cold. So from the first order to the time he got his second bowl, yes, it probably was twenty-six minutes. And if Ellie here says he ordered bean, I can promise you that's what he would

82

have got. And he got it in maybe three minutes of the order. Ellie timed it herself because she knows Mr. Phillips has a hard-on about our service."

"Is that it, Russ?"

"That's it, Mr. Parsons."

Parsons walked back to Phillips. "I've checked on it. You got what you ordered in three minutes or less, not twenty-six. You sent that back and then when you got your next order, you sent it back saying it was cold. So by the time you got your second bowl to your satisfaction, it probably was about twenty minutes or so."

"Is that your answer, Mr. Committee Chairman?"

"That's my answer, Mr. Phillips," said Parsons walking into the hallway that led to the manager's office. To his surprise he found Phillips following him.

Phillips said, "What just happened is typical of what's going on around here. The service is lousy and all we get is excuses. This guy Manders isn't worth a crap! When are you gonna fire his ass, Mr. Chairman?"

"We have no plans to `fire his ass,' Mr. Phillips. He's a good man and any restaurant in town would jump to have him. I believe what he said about your request. I think you're just trying to make him look bad."

Phillips glared at him. "Are you taking the word of a goddamn employee over mine?" His voice was rising. "And a goddamn fag at that?"

Frank said, "Mr. Phillips, this conversation is over."

Phillips followed him down the hallway. "Hey, Mr. Smart Ass, it's over when I say it's over!"

Parsons continued to the end of the hall and turned to open the manager's door. He said nothing.

Phillips yelled after him "You'll be sorry about this, you son of a bitch! You can't walk away from me when I've got legitimate complaints about your lousy grill room service."

Chapter Twenty-six

The Decision

At a special meeting of the board, hastily called by Ashley, not every member showed up, but there was a quorum. Ashley wasted no time.

"Gentlemen, this thing has gone on long enough. We've had our noses bloodied, and now we're gonna fight back. I've asked Dick Kassel to now initiate the steps required for expelling Chet Phillips from the Club. He's done everything we asked him not to, and a lot of other stuff, besides. I don't have to tell you guys. Anyway, Dick Kassel will tell us what happens now."

The attorney cleared his throat. "What happens first is we send Mr. Kassel a letter requesting his presence at a hearing with the purpose of deciding whether or not he should be expelled. The hearing will not be at the Club, probably at our law offices. He is allowed to have his attorney present. I will represent you, if that is your wish.'

He looked at Ashley for approval. The president waved his hand in agreement.

"All right, I'll draft the letter tomorrow, check it out with whomever you name—Larry? And the letter can go out tomorrow, certified mail. I'll plug in the date of the meeting at the very last minute, based on what you gentlemen tell me. I'd like as many of you as possible to tell me right now."

Ten men raised their hands. One more said he'd have to check his travel plans. The attorney looked at Ashley and asked him to get in touch with missing members. The president nodded his yes.

Kassel said, "I'm thinking of July 31 or August 7. That's within the limits set by the bylaws. Those would be the first available dates."

Parsons asked what would happen if Phillips could not make it on the date specified.

"Makes no difference," said Kassel. "The bylaws make it clear he must appear when we say so. There's a reason for that. If there wasn't that stipulation, a member could screw around forever, delaying and delaying. And you men could be sure that Chet Phillips would play it that way.

"One more thing, men," Kassel said. "Even if you all cannot be there, we can hook up a phone conference situation. Now then, a few more items. This hearing, which now is much like a courtroom trial, must be scrupulously fair. Larry, as an attorney, I'd like you to chair. I will conduct the actual formal hearing as your counsel, but I may not run the meeting. It must be a Club member and officer. Phillips must be given every opportunity to answer any charges we make. I also want you to understand we will not go back over any of the issues and get into discussions about them. I will question Mr. Phillips point by point, and based on his answers, a decision will be reached at the end of the meeting as to whether you wish to vote to expel him from your Club."

There were no questions. Ashley declared the meeting over.

x x x x x x

Phone call from Richard Kassel to Chuck Ashley:

"Chuck, I have just had a call from an attorney who apparently is representing Claude Branch. He tells me Branch is preparing to sue Phillips for, among other things, defamation of character. And for making, because of Phillips's letter to all the other clubs in town, it difficult if not impossible for Branch to get another club manager job in this area. I learned, and I'm sure this does not surprise you, that Branch has applied at a number of country clubs. He is finding that the Phillips's letter has hurt him badly."

"I would imagine so, Dick. It's too bad. I had figured Branch would be looking. He's sure taken a beating at our place."

"He sure has, Chuck. I'm guessing he could sue for a ton, I'd think at least a million and a half, probably more."

"That much? Holy balls!"

Letter from Richard Kassel to Chester Phillips;

This is to inform you that a hearing has been scheduled for Thursday, August 7, at 5:30 P.M. in our law offices (address on the letterhead). It will be held in our main conference room.

This hearing is for the purpose of determining whether you should be expelled from membership in Pheasant Ridge Country Club. The hearing will be conducted according to Club bylaws written for this purpose. You are welcome to have your attorney present. The format will be explained to you, and your attorney, if present, at the start of the hearing.

A series of charges will be presented to you as reasons for the expulsion procedure. As required by Club rules, a quorum of the board of governors will be present. At the conclusion of the hearing a vote will be taken, and board members will vote "yes" or "no" as to your expulsion. Neither you nor your attorney may be present as this vote is taken. You will be informed later as to the outcome of the vote.

So that you and your attorney have adequate time to consider the charges that will be made, they will be highlighted here:

1.   Club rules specifically state that no member may reprimand an employee of the Club. You have violated this rule on at least nine specific occasions.

2.   There is a procedure to follow when a Club

85

member feels that a given employee should be reprimanded. You have repeatedly failed to follow this procedure, even after it was specifically called to your attention.

3.　You were informed that you were not to directly contact any Club employee for the purpose of getting information other than matters relating to your own personal account. You have ignored this directive and have continued to contact Club employees—particularly the Club comptroller— for the purpose of getting confidential information as to the personal accounts of other Club members.

4.　After you had accused Mr. Claude Branch of sexual harassment of two employees of the Club, you were told to cease any further investigation on that subject. You were also told that the board would investigate the charges. You have since been told there was no sexual harassment and no charges of sexual harassment have been made by any employee. You ignored the directive.

5.　You have made serious charges against three members of the board, charges that are without substantiation.

6.　After you were directed to withdraw from any issues pertaining to this matter, you wrote two separate letters to all board members. You also wrote two separate letters to all members of the Club. The problems arising from these letters are significant. Your letters contained statements not supported by facts and have caused discomfort and embarrassment to the people involved.
Although it is a separate issue, you have surely libeled the people involved.

7.　Not only did you circulate your letters to all Club members, you mailed copies to the various presidents of other clubs in the area, numbering at least 10. You also mailed a copy to the mayor of Bridgeside. This, too, has caused discomfort and embarrassment to the officers and board members involved. The damage to these individuals and the Club itself is incalculable.

8.　It has been brought to our attention that you caused checks to be written to two Club employees, a violation not only of Club policy, but an act surely against the spirit of the philosophy on which a Club must operate.

Each of these issues will be addressed in the hearing.
We will expect you at the hearing on the date and time here specified. Your attorney is of course free to contact me in advance of the hearing. Further, you are hereby directed not to disclose the fact of this meeting, its time,

place and purpose, to anyone outside your immediate family.

This is a serious meeting with a serious objective. It is completely confidential in nature, a fact we will assume you will honor and adhere to.

Sincerely,

Richard Kassel, attorney-at-law

x x x x x x

Phone call from Chester Phillips to attorney Fred Webber:

"Fred, Chet. Those bastards have sent me a letter telling me they're gonna expel me! I want to sue their asses!"

"Chet, calm down. First of all, I'm not your attorney any more. Remember? Second, they can't expel you without a hearing. I'm sure the letter tells you about a hearing. They're not stupid, and sure as hell their attorney isn't. Read the letter again; I'm sure it's about a hearing."

"Yeah, it's a hearing. But it says it's for the purpose of expelling me, for Christ's sake!"

"I doubt that's what it says, but if it makes you happy to think so, go ahead."

"Well, anyway, Fred, I don't like it. Why can't we sue them?"

"Chet, I told you this would happen if you kept charging ahead. I told you to back off. You didn't. They have every right to do this. They could expel you on any one of several issues, for God's sake!"

"Well, they want me to be there on August 7. I can't make that."

"Chet, again, I remind you I'm not your attorney. But I'll tell you right now, yes, you've got to make that date. I've read their bylaws. Gives them the right to set the date. You have no choice. You must appear when they say you must. That bylaw rule is there for a specific reason. Whatever you think you're going to be doing on August 7, change your plans. Period."

"Shit! Well, mark your calendar for the 7th of August."

"Chet, how many times do I have to tell you? I'm not your goddamn attorney!"

"So you won't do it? You're abandoning me?"

"Oh, for Christ's sake, Chet. I told you before, cut that crap out. You've not taken my advice on this thing. You've ignored it. You think you're God. Impregnable. Well, you're not. They're coming after you and they have every right to do so!"

"Then I've got no lawyer. What the hell do I do?"

"I can recommend one of our young guys. Or, you can go to another law firm."

"Fred, you can't do that!"

"Oh yes I can. I have. Do you want the name of one of

our guys or not?"

"I don't want some young punk. You drop me, Fred, and I'll sue your ass!"

"Now listen, you asshole! You want to sue me, be my guest. Good-bye."

Chapter Twenty-seven

The Complainers

While the Phillips problem was continuing, with all its irritation and frustration, Parsons had continued with his up-dating and remodeling plan. His committee had spent many hours going over every idea advanced by the decorator, and one by one each of several issues was resolved. The board had approved the plan for the restrooms, and because the construction involved turned out to be relatively minor, both the men's and women's rooms were now complete.

The decorator had shown the committee several different wallpaper styles and because this kind of thing is intensely personal, Parsons allowed far more discussion than he normally would have. After a considerable amount of time, the small group had agreed on the paper for both rooms. One of the women who had served on a previous house committee had a thought.

"Guys, I was on the committee five years ago when we did the men's and women's locker rooms. I can tell you we had more problems with the damn wall paper than anything else. Everybody's an expert. And what one person loves, another hates. And boy, do the haters complain! So you might as well accept it, some of our members, particularly some of my women friends, I must admit, will give us a bad time."

"Yes, I understand that," said Frank. Do you have any words of wisdom for us, Katie?" He liked the woman; she was smart and had been a strong committee member.

"I'm not sure about the wisdom of it, but my best advice is just to make our decision, go ahead with it, and then expect some bitches from the—excuse me—bitches."

The committee then agreed on two designs, one for each restroom. The paper hangers arrived two days later and by the end of the day, both restrooms were finished.

At 8:30 the next morning, Frank got a phone call at his home. No one who knew him ever called before 9, so he knew the call was not a friend.

"Mr. Parsons, this is Mabel Bauer? You're the House Committee chairman, right?"

"That's right, Mrs. Bauer, what can I do for you?"

"Well, you can take down that horrid paper in the women's restroom. It's awful, just awful. No one likes it. It must come down."

"Gee, Mrs. Bauer, our committee liked it fine. We looked at dozens of designs, and this is the one we all agreed on."

"Well, I'd like to know the names of the people on your committee."

"Yes, Mrs. Bauer. Their names are in the roster book, but I'll give them to you." He read their names.

"Well, you all must have terrible taste, Mr. Parsons. And we want that paper taken down right away."

"Oh, come now, Mrs. Bauer, surely you can't mean that. The paper just went up. Let's live with it awhile. Let's see how others feel. I'm sure you agree that wallpaper is a very personal thing."

"Well, all I agree on is that paper is horrid. It should come down."

"Mrs. Bauer, I can't do that. I'm sure you understand."

"Well, you are some committee chairman!"

"Thank you, Mrs. Bauer."

He said aloud, "My God, she thought about that call all night!"

x x x x x x

With the golf course at Pheasant Ridge now moving into late season, activity at the Club now was at its yearly peak. There were more men eating lunch then changing clothes to go out on the course. Wives met for lunch, bridge, and morning golf. Much of the talk was about the Phillips' situation, and Parsons tried hard to stay clear of it. When people asked him what he knew, he only told them the matter was confidential. The frequently repeated question, which he also avoided, had to do with whether he thought the board would expel Phillips. Everyone seemed to know there was a formal hearing scheduled.

How these confidential matters seemed to regularly leak out, no matter how much and how often board members had been urged to keep their mouths shut, was a mystery to him. He figured most of it was because board members, coming home after a long and frustrating meeting, would confide in their wives.

Even more of a mystery was how Phillips could find out that a board meeting was being held on a given night outside the clubhouse at a restaurant. But Phillips had found out. His sources of information were several, and it was obvious there were still employees who were feeding him material.

One of Parsons's fairly good friends constantly poked at him about Club matters. His number one topic had to do with Russ Manders. "Is he really queer, Frank?"

x x x x x x

As the club remodeling project continued, Frank got several calls. Most of the calls had to do with small details. "How come there are only two urinals in the men's restroom?" "What happened to the pictures that used to hang in the lobby?" "Are you going to replace that awful rug in the lounge?" "What happens to the furniture we have now?" "Why was the picture of Sam Snead and Ben Hogan moved from the grill room?"

Parsons realized that each member deserved an answer, and he did the best he could, but the business of committee chair was getting to him, he had to admit.

x x x x x x

Again at about 8:30 one morning (Why were all the calls made so early in the day? he thought), a man called. It was a fellow he knew slightly.

"Mr. Parsons, ah, Frank, what the hell is going on at the thirteenth tee? What are you guys thinking?"

"Jim, I'm not on the Golf Committee. That's really not my area of responsibility."

"Well, you ought to know about that. If a guy on the board can't answer that question, that's a helluva note!"

Chapter Twenty-eight

Attorneys, Letters, and Phone Calls

Phone call from Cory Phillips to his father:

"Dad, it's Cory. Well, I hear they're going to expel you. I told you what would happen. I've resigned from the Club, as I told you I would, but everybody's talking about it."

"Cory, I told you before it's none of your business. But don't worry about me, I've still got a few tricks up my sleeve."

"Dad, that figures. For once in your life, Dad, face facts. Tricks aren't going to save you. Admit you were wrong and throw yourself on their mercy."

"Cory, this conversation is over."

Phone call from Cory Phillips to attorney Fred Webber:

"Mr. Webber, this is Cory Phillips, Chester Phillips' son."

"Yes, Cory, what can I do for you? I'm no longer your dad's attorney, you know."

"Well, sir, I'm calling to see if there's anything you can do about getting my father out of trouble. He's going to hurt our whole family, and he's going to hurt himself most."

"Cory, I appreciate your concern and I respect you for the way you want to help your dad, but I'm afraid there's nothing I can do. Your father is a very determined person. He didn't listen to my advice and that's why I'm no longer his lawyer."

"Well, sir, can you get him another lawyer? From your firm, maybe?"

"I could do that, Cory, but I already offered that and he turned me down. I'll give you a name and you can call the fellow. He's young but he's pretty smart. I don't know whether he'll do it or not, so call him and find out what he says."

"All right, sir. Thank you. Do you think my dad has a chance?"

"In plain English, Cory, no, not a chance."

Letter from Claude Branch to Charles Ashley:

Dear Mr. Ashley:

I understand that the hearing on Mr. Phillips is scheduled for August 7. I also understand that my participation in this hearing is not required.

Regardless of the outcome of the hearing, I am advising you that it is my intention to sue Mr. Phillips. My attorney has asked me to advise you of this, although it is a separate issue from your hearing procedure.

Mr. Phillips has caused me and my family considerable mental stress and physical pain, to say nothing of the charges by him that have made it virtually impossible for me to find Club employment in this part of the country. I'm sure you understand that in view of what has happened at Pheasant Ridge, my continued position there as manager is not something I can plan on.

I wanted you to get this information directly from me rather than have it blindside you in some other way. It is my intent to stay at the Club as long as you need me and until I find a suitable club position elsewhere.

Thank you for your support and personal kindness the past several years.

Sincerely,

Claude Branch

x x x x x x

Phone call from Chet Phillips to Fred Webber:

"Fred, this is Chet. I understand you ...."

"Just a minute, Chet. I've told you, I'm not your attorney. We've crossed that bridge. Anything you have to say about this matter is irrelevant. I have no interest in it."

"Goddammit, Fred, you can't do this!"

"Yes, I can. Now let's get this over with. I've got lots of work in front of me."

"Okay, you son of a bitch! Did you give my son Cory the name of an attorney?"

"Yes, I did."

"Is he any good?"

"Oh, for God's sake, Chet, knock it off. Goodbye."

"You asshole!" yelled Phillips to a dead phone.

Kassel called Costello and the two agreed to meet over lunch to discuss the hearing, now just days away.

Kassel began, "Larry, as an attorney yourself, you are as aware as I am that this hearing absolutely must follow strict procedure. Phillips' attorney will be primed for anything we do that is out of line. Now you're going to be the presiding officer, per the bylaws. This means you'll open the meeting, state the ground rules, and make it clear that as the presiding officer it is your responsibility to run the meeting, to keep it on track and not to take sides. Is there anything you want to ask me about any of this?"

"No, Dick, I think I've got it pretty well. One thing, what is the role of Phillips' lawyer? Where does he fit in?"

"First, I want you to know I've learned Fred Webber is no longer representing Phillips. He quit. I'm sure he had every reason to. Second, he got one of his firm's young lawyers to work with Chet. He got this lawyer because of the efforts of Cory, Chet's son. I learned this from Cory himself. Now I don't know this young attorney. But if he's any good, he'll come at this thing from a different angle. Different, I mean, from the way Fred Webber would have done it. I think he'll plead he's just new at this thing and needs time to study it. In other words, he'll ask for a delay. I emphasize that this cannot be granted. It's a smart play, if he does it—I certainly would—but we can't let it happen.

"Because this new man is young and just hired, he will use that as a strength. Again, I would. You'll have to be extraordinarily careful and fair, as I know you'll be. However, be very formal throughout. Give him no reasons for accusing us of coming in with a loaded deck. Show understanding of his probable pitch that he is not really familiar with the situation, but in the end, don't go overboard. His late arrival on the scene is tough on him, and perhaps tough on his client, but it has no bearing on the matter. I know you know that.

"Make it clear that once they start, I mean Chet and his attorney, they will not be interrupted. Answer any question either of them may have as briefly as you can. Don't go beyond the literal scope of the question. Use me when you wish. I will deal with issues having to do with the bylaws. You, on the other hand, deal only with issues that have impact on the hearing itself. If Phillips gets nasty, and I'll be amazed if he doesn't, it is your responsibility to calm him down. I know you'll do that very well. Keep constantly in mind that this is a hearing for a specific purpose, and only one purpose. If the vote goes against him, he is expelled from the Club without recourse. In other words, and again, I know you know this, he cannot reapply at some future time. If he's voted out, he's out! Period. Fred Webber knew that, but perhaps the new lawyer will not. And so he may try to work that issue a little, looking for some loophole. No way. There ain't no loophole."

"Okay Dick, I think I'm on top of it. Oh, yeah, one more thing. What about Phillips's threat to sue the Club? `To sue our ass,' his favorite expression?"

"Larry, I suppose technically, he can sue us. Sadly, in the U.S. today just about anyone can sue anyone for just about anything. Could he win a suit? Very doubtful. And particularly so if the hearing is run by the book. Otherwise, Phillips has no case. In fact, and keep this in mind, the Club could surely sue him, and I think you'd win. The publicity could be bad, and the press would play it up for sure, but you'd win. I doubt you want to go that route, however. Right?"

"Right. All we want is for this thing to be over. One more thing and I'm through asking questions. I ask this question for two reasons: one, I'm interested from the Club's point of view, and two, I'm interested as an attorney. How much do you feel our legal bill is going to run?"

Kassel smiled. "Well, first, I haven't seen the most recent figures. My fee is pretty substantial, as you know. And I've had some of our assistants doing research, not just of bylaws, but of similar cases with other clubs.

94

This is an estimate, Larry, but to date, you're well over $40,000 in fees."

Phone call from Chet Phillips to Fred Webber:

"Fred, this is Chet. Yeah, I know you're not my attorney, I wanted you to know that prick Branch is suing me! Can he do that? I want to counter-sue. How much can he sue for and expect to get it? This suit is for $2.5 million, for Christ's sake!"

"Dammit, Chet, stop calling me! Stop already! I'm not your fucking attorney. How much can he sue for? Anything his lawyer thinks he can get. I think the figure of $2.5 million is completely justified. You've ruined his career, for God's sake!"

"Holy shit!"

Letter from Russell Manders to Frank Parsons, copy to Charles Ashley:

Dear Mr. Parsons:

I understand that a hearing on Mr. Phillips is scheduled for August 7. I understand that I am not a participant in this hearing.

This letter is to advise you that I am suing Mr. Phillips. My attorney advised me to inform you of this as a matter of courtesy, although my situation with Mr. Phillips is a separate issue.

Mr. Phillips has caused me, my family, and my brother considerable pain and stress. His charges against me, unproved and unsubstantiated, have made it difficult for me to carry out my responsibilities at the Club. Should I leave the Club to seek employment elsewhere, it may prove difficult for me to secure a position at some other Club as manager, which is my goal.

You and other officers have been very helpful to me, Mr.Parsons, and I wanted you to know I appreciate it.

Sincerely,

Russell Manders

Phone call from Frank Parsons to Larry Costello:

"Larry, Frank Parsons. I have a letter from Russ Manders. He's suing Chet Phillips. I know you're going to run the hearing, so I wanted you to know this. Chuck Ashley knows it, too."

Phone call from Larry Costello to Richard Kassel:

"Dick, Larry Costello. I just hear that Russ Manders, our restaurant manager, is suing Chet Phillips. I don't know who his lawyer is, but I'd imagine Branch's lawyer along with Manders's, will be getting together to get their facts straight. And of course, Phillips's new lawyer will know about this by the time of the hearing."

"Thanks, Larry. I appreciate knowing this. Phillips has

got himself a boatload of trouble."

"Has Manders got a case?"

"I would certainly think so. Almost as good a case as Claude Branch. And there's the homosexual angle. The right jury these days might give him double just for that."

Phone call from Chester Phillips to Attorney Robert Newhouse:

"Newhouse, this is Mr. Phillips. I've got an idea. I'd like you to play heavily on the fact that I've been a big contributor to the club. Money and lots of my personal time and a former officer. That ought to help."

"Well, sir, I don't mean to be negative, but I don't see that as a plus. In fact, it could be a minus. They will hold that you of all people should have known better than to do as you did."

"Shit! Boy, you are negative, all right. You better not go into this hearing that way."

"Sir, I won't. I'm looking for every angle I can find. But you have to be realistic, sir. You hurt several people. You made it very difficult for some employees to do their jobs. You yelled at them in front of other employees. You attacked the Club president, both personally and professionally. He's a very popular man, from all I gather. You accused the House Chairman of wrong-doing, of dishonesty. He's been in the Club as long as you have, and he's popular and well thought-of. And you've attacked the entire board in one way or another. Realistically, sir, I don't feel you have a lot of pluses going for you."

"Well, goddammit, Newhouse, find something. That's what I'm paying you for!"

"Yes, sir."

Chapter Twenty-nine

The Hearing

August 7 in the law offices of Richard Kassel's firm: The room was a typical business conference room. There was a long table with chairs on each side, as many as twenty of them. Windows overlooked the downtown area, with late afternoon commuter traffic now building. There were no photos on the walls. There were several pitchers of water and a large bowl filled with ice cubes.

At exactly 5:15 P.M. a young woman entered the room with two uniformed maintenance men. The two men moved the table away from the windows and in the space left placed another table, so that in effect, there was a T-shape. They then placed all of the chairs on one side of the table and put two more chairs on the opposite side at the end of the T. The young woman carefully inspected the layout, speaking in a low tone to the two men. The woman then placed a yellow pad of paper on the table in front of each chair. She put a pencil alongside each pad. She inspected the layout once more, then left the room. She came back in less than a minute with Kassel.

"Is this the way you wanted it, sir?"

"Yes, thank you, Jennifer. Good job as usual." He smiled at her. "Well, I think we're all set."

As Kassel left the conference room to go back to his office to get his files, he stopped where a man was sitting just outside the main room. He nodded to the man and spoke quietly, asking a question. The man, dressed in a dark suit and sturdily built, smiled and patted his suit pocket where there was an obvious bulge.

At 5:20 P.M. Chester Phillips walked into the room. On his face, once again, was the mirthless smile. Within seconds Kassel came back carrying two very thick files in both hands. He nodded to Phillips but did not speak. Within another few minutes, four members of the board arrived, then two more. Kassel indicated they could sit where they wished. He asked Phillips to take a seat at the end of the T. Phillips, carrying a thick file himself, sat down without speaking. Ashley came in and smiled at board members and Kassel had him sit not at the head of the main table but a little to one side.

Parsons walked in and seconds later, three more board members. Kassel pointed out to them where they could sit. Two more arrived, and seconds later one more. The total was now fourteen of the sixteen members. Two would not be able to make it.

At 5:29, Phillips's attorney, Robert Newhouse, came in and was directed to a seat next to Phillips. At exactly 5:30 Costello, seated in the center of the main table and directly opposite Phillips, looked at his watch and began to speak.

"I am calling this meeting to order. As secretary of the Club, I am declaring we have a quorum of the Pheasant Ridge Board of Governors." He directed his next comment to a woman who had, without anyone really taking note of her, come in and taken a seat well away from the table.

Costello said to her, "You may put your machine on the table in front of you. I assume it is plugged in?"

The woman nodded, saying nothing.

"All right, thank you. For the information of all present, this woman is the official court reporter of this meeting. Everything that is said will be recorded by her, plus anything that I, as chair of the meeting, request that she note.

"Let me explain the procedure here this afternoon. I have been asked as secretary of the Club, and as a practicing attorney, to chair the meeting, or rather, the hearing. My job is to see that we stay on the subject, that we do not stray into time-consuming nonpertinent issues. Mr. Richard Kassel will conduct the questions pertinent to the hearing itself. That is not my role.

"This hearing is to determine whether Mr. Chester Phillips should be expelled from membership in Pheasant Ridge Country Club. The hearing will be conducted along lines set out many years ago by the then board of governors of the Club. The hearing will be formal but not rigidly so. All questions should be directed to me. If you wish to speak, raise your hand and I will recognize you. However, I would ask that you limit your questions strictly to issues that are pertinent.

"The charges against Mr. Phillips will be specified by our attorney, Mr. Kassel here, and I will shortly turn over the meeting to him. For the benefit of all of you but particularly Mr. Phillips and his attorney, Mr. Newhouse, while Mr. Kassel will be conducting the questions pertaining to the charges, Mr. Kassel is not—repeat not—in charge of the hearing. I am. And I will rule on all questions and points that are either not clear or might be argued. This is strictly according to our bylaws. Mr. Newhouse, is that point clear to you? And is it clear to you, Mr. Phillips?"

Both men nodded.

"Mr. Phillips, at the close of the presentation of the Club's charges, you and your attorney will be given all the time you wish to respond. There is no time limit to this hearing. I will do my very best to be professional and to be fair to both sides. After the hearing is concluded and Mr. Phillips has been given ample time to respond as he wishes, Mr. Phillips and his attorney will be asked to leave the room. Gentlemen, you will wish to leave and go home at that point. Specifically, and according to the rules, you must leave the premises. You may not wait in the corridor or anyplace else.

"At that juncture the matter of the hearing will be discussed by the board and the vote taken. For your information, Mr. Ashley has recused himself from voting. He need not have done that, but he chose to do so. The vote need not be unanimous. A simple majority is all that is required."

Costello paused and looked around the room. "Thank you, we are ready to proceed. I will now turn this hearing over to Mr. Kassel."

x x x x x x

Richard Kassel checked his first file folder and spoke to Phillips. "Sir,

I understand that you are here representing yourself, and that your attorney is also here, being Mr. Newhouse. Is this correct?"

Phillips nodded. "Yes. Ah, Mr. Kassel, may I ask a question?"

"Yes, you may, but if your question is one of procedure, I would ask you to direct it to Mr. Costello."

Phillips nodded and turned to Costello. Again the mirthless smile appeared. "A question, Mr. Costello?"

"Go ahead, Mr. Phillips."

"Is this a hearing stacked against me? Have I got a fair shot? Or is this some kind of kangaroo court?"

Shocked, Robert Newhouse immediately spoke. "Mr. Costello, that question is withdrawn by my client. Repeat, withdrawn. Your instructions and explanation were both perfectly clear. We come into this hearing with the assumption it will be fair and impartial. We respect your ability to run the meeting that way. We respect Mr. Kassel's professionalism. I regret my client's remark. I'm sure he does too. Thank you."

The young man looked sharply at Phillips, who shrugged his shoulders. Board members exchanged glances, but no one spoke.

Kassel, his tone flat and cold, took up where he had left off.

"Mr. Phillips, you are aware of the purpose of this hearing. I am going to direct a series of questions to you and will ask for a response to each question. The questions will be completely relevant and in accordance with the letter sent to you earlier. Your specific responses to each question will be appreciated."

Kassel glanced meaningfully at Newhouse, who nodded and turned his head to look at his client. Again Phillips shrugged his shoulders.

Kassel, now looking directly at Phillips and his voice still cold, said, "Mr. Phillips, you have charged that the Club manager, Mr. Claude Branch, sexually harassed two female employees of the Club. Mr. Phillips, are you an expert in sexual harassment in this state?"

"No, I'm not an expert at anything, I guess. But I know sexual harassment when I see it."

"Just a minute, sir. You have answered my question that you are not an expert in this particular field. That is enough, sir. But your additional statement brings up an entirely new point. Did you see sexual harassment take place? Your statement would seem to imply that you did. If so this is entirely new information. Did you see any sexual harassment, sir?"

"No, I guess I didn't actually see it, but I was told it happened."

"Sir, I would point out to you that what you may have seen and what you may have been told are two totally different issues. Your answer to the question asked is that you are not an expert in sexual harassment. Let me ask you further, have you read any of the laws on sexual harassment in this state?"

"No, I guess I haven't."

"Mr. Phillips, it is not necessary, nor do I consider it an adequate answer for you to use the phrase `I guess.' I will ask your attorney to advise you to refrain from using `I guess' as an answer to any question." He flashed a look at Newhouse. Newhouse, in obvious anger put his hand on Chet arm. "Mr. Phillips, you are so advised."

Kassel, irritated but not showing it, continued. "Mr. Phillips, you have previously been told that we would thoroughly investigate your charges of sexual harassment. We have done that. Neither of the two women you charge were harassed has ever stated that she was harassed. They have flatly and repeatedly denied it. Furthermore, we have spoken at length with other office personnel and no one—repeat, no one—observed any sexual harassment. We are completely satisfied that no sexual harassment took place. Mr. Branch is innocent of your charge. We consider this matter settled and done."

Again the smirk appeared on Phillips's face. "You got to them, didn't you?"

Kassel struggled to stay calm and detached. "Mr. Phillips, you do yourself no service by speaking that way. I will again ask you to confine your answers to the questions asked. Mr. Newhouse, I again request that you advise your client to refrain from his ad lib comments. They are out of line and contribute nothing to this hearing. I also ask that Mr. Costello so advise you."

Costello immediately spoke up. "Mr. Phillips, ah, Chet, come on, what you are doing is not right and will not be further accepted. I ask the court reporter to take note of this."

The woman nodded a silent *yes.*

Robert Newhouse, looking straight at Kassel, said, "We acknowledge, Mr. Kassel, that Mr. Phillips is not an expert in the field of sexual harassment. We acknowledge that he never saw sexual harassment take place. We further acknowledge that is totally inappropriate to suggest that you or anyone else connected with the Club influenced these two women to say anything but the truth."

Kassel cleared his throat. "We will now proceed to the next issue, Mr. Phillips. This has to do with the Club rule that no member may reprimand an employee. May I ask you if you have read that rule, sir?"

"Not recently."

Kassel, his mouth set in a thin line, paused. Most board members felt he was close to blowing, but they admired his self-control.

"Is it your answer, Mr. Phillips, that you have not read the rule at all, or have read it, but not recently?"

"As I said, not recently. I may have read it in the past."

"I see. Well, if you have not read it recently, when exactly did you read it? Several months? Years? Never, maybe?"

"I don't remember."

"For the record," and Kassel nodded pointedly to the court reporter, "Have you ever read the rule? Yes or no?"

"I've already told you, Mr. Attorney, I don't remember. Probably not for a long time."

Kassel looked at Newhouse, who said, "For the record, Mr. Kassel, we acknowledge that my client has never read the rule."

Kassel said, "Thank you, Mr. Newhouse. For the record, the rule states very clearly that no member may reprimand an employee, and if a member feels an employee is not behaving properly or not providing the expected service, the member is to speak or write to the chair of the House Committee and register the complaint in that matter. Mr. Phillips, did you speak or write to the chair of the house committee about your feelings about Mr. Branch?"

"I talked to the House Committee chair about the restaurant manager. The chairman wasn't interested, I guess."

"Mr. Phillips, the question has to do with your reprimanding of any given employee. This includes Mr. Branch and Mr. Manders, and any other Club employee. Now then, Mr. Phillips, did you at any time reprimand Mr. Branch, either to Mr. Branch alone or in front of other employees?"

"I spoke to Mr. Branch man-to-man."

"Man to man? We have the testimony of four employees who work in the Club office that you upbraided Mr. Branch while standing in his office door, that you did so in a loud voice, that you accused him of being lazy, coming in to work late, not running a tight ship, and that you did this not once, but at least three times in front of the office staff."

"Like I said, man-to-man. He's a grown-up. He should be able to take that."

"Take that, sir? Taking being remonstrated in front of his own staff people? Doing it in a loud voice? Calling him, among other things, `lazy'? Do you really feel that was man-to-man? Do you honestly state that you did not reprimand Mr. Branch?"

"I consider what I did to be strictly man-to-man. There was no reprimand."

"All right, Mr. Phillips. What about speaking or writing to the House Committee chair?"

"I didn't think he'd be interested. I thought he'd walk away like he did another time about the restaurant service."

"One item at a time, sir. I specifically asked you if you talked to or wrote to the committee chair about Mr. Branch. I will ask that question again."

"I wrote to lots of people about Mr. Branch."

"Yes, you certainly did that," said Kassel dryly. But the question was did you write the House Committee chair?"

"No, I didn't."

"Did you write or speak to any member of the House Committee about Mr. Branch?"

"I don't know who's on the House Committee?"

"That, sir, would appear to answer the question, however obscurely."

Newhouse raised his hand. "We acknowledge, Mr. Kassel, that Mr. Phillips did not take his complaint to the House Committee or any member of the committee."

Phillips turned angrily to his attorney. "Whose side are you on, for God's sake?"

"I'm on your side, Mr. Phillips, and I'm trying to do my best for you. Frankly, sir, you are hurting your own case with your answers."

Kassel again took up his questioning. "After you were told that the rules of the Club did not permit reprimanding employees, did you again do that? Reprimand one or more employees?

"I don't consider what I did `reprimanding.'"

Kassel turned to Costello. "I think this is an instance, Mr. Secretary, that calls for a response from you."

Costello said, "Mr. Phillips—Chet—please try to cooperate. We call it `reprimanding,' and you keep insisting you were talking `man-to-man. People who heard you, reliable witnesses, called it `reprimanding,' and two of them used words like `harassing,' and `intimidating.' You did so in a loud voice; furthermore, you acknowledge, through your attorney, that you made no attempt to write the House Committee chairman or anyone on the House Committee. I am going to make a decision here that one, you did indeed publicly reprimand Mr. Branch at least once, and after you were specifically directed not to, you did it again. On the basis of what I have heard, it's clear you violated Club rules, and you did it knowingly and deliberately. With this decision made, Mr. Kassel, please proceed with the hearing."

Kassel turned back to his file. He looked quickly at his watch and turned to Costello with an inquiring look. "Mr. Secretary, I just noticed it's nearly seven. I had no idea the time was moving so fast. This is up to you, but do you think it might be time to take a break? I know there is a box dinner of some kind that has been ordered. What do you think?"

Costello said,"I think you're right. Let's take a dinner break. Is there someone you have to notify to get the dinners?"

Kassel immediately got up and left the room, and Costello told the members, and Phillips, and his attorney that a break was in order and that a box lunch would be served soon. Neither Phillips nor Newhouse said anything.

x x x x x x

The board members got up, stretched their arms and legs, indulged in small talk, and waited for the meals to appear. Several went to the men's room. In walking out of the conference room, they noticed the man in the dark suit. Apparently he had been sitting there throughout the entire session. He was a burly man and seemed out of place. He said nothing, but nodded to one or two of the board members who walked by him.

One board member said to Costello, "Who the hell is that guy sitting back there?"

Costello smiled. "He's a security man. An off-duty cop. We hired him for the evening."

The board member's eyes opened wide. "You mean what I think you mean? That you felt something might happen we'd need a guy like that?"

"That's what I mean."

"Wow! Is he armed?"

"You got it," said Costello.

x x x x x x

By 7:45 everyone present had eaten, and Costello, looking pointedly at his watch, said, "Gentlemen, let's resume. Please get back to your places.

The members quickly took their seats. Phillips, who had been in a fairly heated conversation with his attorney, also sat down. His face was red and his lips were set in a thin line.

"Mr. Kassel," said Costello, "you have the floor."

Kassel nodded and began again. "We will now move on to the next issue. Mr. Phillips, after you had reprimanded Mr. Branch openly in front of several Club employees, it was called to your attention that this behavior on your part was against Club policy. You were directed, via a letter from the president, to either follow the procedure or completely withdraw from the situation. Just before we broke for dinner, the club secretary ruled on the basis of your testimony that you had violated club policy and that you did it knowingly and deliberately. Further, that you did not follow Club policy and call to the attention of the House Committee chairman that you had a complaint against the Club manager, Mr. Branch.

"Now, sir, I'd like to ask you if, after being told to have no further contact with any Club employee on matters other than your own bill, you went ahead and continued contact with several employees. Is this true?"

"Would you repeat the question?"

102

"Certainly. You were told to have no further contact with Club employees in the office, other than questions or issues relating to your own bill. Did you follow that direction, sir?"

"I saw that nothing was being done about my complaints. I saw that, as usual, I'd have to take matters into my own hands."

"Mr. Phillips, the question was did you continue to have contact with office employees after you were directed not to?"

"I suppose so."

"You suppose so? I'll take that as a `yes.'" Kassel turned to Costello, who nodded and said, "For the purpose of keeping this hearing moving and on track, I'll make this ruling. From now on, any answers from Mr. Phillips requiring either a `yes' or a `no' will be taken as a `yes' when answered by anything but a flat `no.' Mr. Newhouse, do you understand the ruling, and do you have any comment about it?"

Newhouse said "Yes, I understand the ruling. I agree with it. And again I ask my client to answer the questions precisely, leaving no room for interpretation." This time the lawyer did not look at Phillips.

Kassel said, "Thank you, sir. Now then, Mr. Phillips, in spite of the direction given you, it's established that you continued to contact people in the Club office, specifically the comptroller who has access to all the financial records of Club member's accounts. Our investigation indicates you contacted this person at least seven more times after you were directed not to. Our investigation shows that you asked for—and got—the billing records of Mr. Ashley. Is that correct?"

"I previously had some of Mr. Ashley's records. The other times, I just got some additional stuff that was pertinent."

"Mr. Phillips, I'll take that as a `yes.' Recorder, please note. Now, after being told not to, did you also ask for—and get—the billing information about Mr. Parsons?"

"Yes, I did. I had been told he was pulling a fast one, and I wanted to have the facts. I had learned that in his capacity as House Chairman, he was getting free refreshments at committee meetings. That's cheating the members of the Club, and I won't stand for that!"

"Mr. Phillips, your answer is `yes', you did ask for and get information about Mr. Parsons after being told not to. Please note this, recorder.

"Next question on the same issue. Did you, after being told not to have further contact with your source in the Club office then ask for the billing records of Mr. Costello? And please note, sir, that this question clearly calls for a `yes' or `no' and does not require an explanation on your part. I remind you that you will have ample opportunity to speak after our questions are all asked. And answered."

Phillips allowed himself a familiar smirk, and said, "I guess, under the restrictions that have been placed on me, my answer has to be yes to that particular question."

"Thank you, Mr. Phillips. For the record, let us note that in the case of three separate members of the Club and the board, you asked for and got information as to their billing—even though you had been told not to request such information."

Phillips shrugged his shoulders.

Kassel allowed himself a small sigh. "Mr. Phillips, I'll move on to the next point. A Club employee who is in charge of maintenance was contacted by you some time ago. You had called him and visited him in his apartment. Is this true?"

"Yes, it is true. I had heard some things about the remodeling project. I wanted to see if they were true."

"Is it true that this particular Club employee had told you he had nothing to say to you, and that he, in fact, had specifically asked you not to come to his home?"

"He may have said that. I don't remember."

"For your information this person does say he told you exactly that— not to come to his home. Is he right?"

"Yes, I went to see him at his home, ah, his apartment."

"You asked this man, Bill Gomez, several questions about the renovating project, is that right?"

"Yes, that's right. It was not several questions, it was just two or three."

"I stand corrected," said Kassel dryly. "All right, two or three questions. Did you ask him for information specifically about the sexual orientation of the decorator hired for the Club job?"

"You're damn right I did. They hired a damn queer!"

"That would be a `yes'. Mr. Phillips, my facts show that you asked Mr. Gomez several questions, but I won't dwell on that. The facts available to me tell me that Mr. Gomez told you he thought that the issue of the decorator had to do with competency rather than sexual orientation. Is that right? Did he say that?"

"He might have, I don't remember."

"All right, it's not really important except in a general sense. This question, however, is important. You told Mr. Gomez that you were a member of a `secret' committee formed to make a special investigation. I ask you, what is that `secret' committee, who formed it, and how did you become a member?"

"You're asking me who is on the committee?"

"No, sir, that is the one question I did not ask you. I am asking you three other questions on that subject. What is the committee, who formed it, and how did you become a member?"

"I can't remember who formed it. I'm on it because it is well-known that I am for the best interests of the Club."

"Mr. Phillips, that answer begs the question, and I am asking your attorney to particularly note the fact. Mr. Phillips, let's be realistic and honest with each other. Is it possible there is no committee? That you told Mr. Gomez you represented a `secret' committee in order to give some weight to your request? Isn't it a fact that the only member of this `committee' is you?"

"There are some other people on it."

"Who, Mr. Phillips? Who?"

"I don't remember. The committee was formed some time ago."

"I see. When was the last meeting of the committee?"

"I don't remember. A while ago, I guess."

"Mr. Phillips, I am a patient man. This hearing is based on patience and fairness. You, however, are not only testing the will of the people sitting around this table, but in all honesty, I must tell you that you are doing yourself no good. No good at all. My take on this `committee' based on your extremely vague answers, is that there is no `committee,' there never was a `committee', and that the `committee' is simply a device, your invention if you please, to be used as a kind of tactical weapon to help you get information."

Kassel turned to Costello. "Mr. Secretary, based on the lack of specifics here and the nature of Mr. Phillips's answers, I am asking you to make a ruling here so that we can get on with the hearing."

Costello cleared his throat. "Mr. Phillips, from the beginning our intent is to be fair and impartial in this matter. However, it requires cooperation on your part. I have listened carefully to your responses on this particular issue, and I can find nothing that indicates the existence of any committee formed to get privileged information from a given employee. Unless you have anything specific to add to this matter, unless you can answer—now—Mr. Kassel's questions, I am going to rule there is no committee and never was. Do you have a response?"

Phillips shrugged and said nothing.

Costello said to Kassel. "All right, Mr. Kassel, let us proceed."

Kassel, remaining outwardly cool, said, "At his apartment, you apparently told Mr. Gomez that he was duty-bound to answer your questions. Is that true?"

"I don't remember. I might have said something like that?"

"You apparently told Mr. Gomez that if he did not answer, you would take legal action against him."

"Legal action?"

"Yes, sir. Did you or did you not threaten Mr. Gomez with a lawsuit if he did not answer your questions?"

"I don't remember threatening him."

"Mr. Phillips, Mr. Gomez has told us that you said you were prepared to spend upwards of $150,000 of your own money on your investigation. Is this correct?"

"You're the one saying so, Mr. Attorney."

"No, sir, I am the one asking you, Mr. Phillips. We have a sworn statement by Mr. Gomez that you specifically mentioned a figure of $150,000. That you specifically threatened a lawsuit against him, that you asked him not two or three questions, but several, and that you specifically mentioned a `secret' committee. Finally, that your attitude was not only intimidating but threatening, and that you used this attitude in an attempt to scare him into answering."

Phillips looked at his attorney. On his lips was the half smile now familiar to everyone present. He spoke to his attorney but his answer was obviously directed at Richard Kassel. "You see, Newhouse? I told you this hearing would go this way. I told you I'd be examined and questioned like a fucking criminal. And my question to you, Newhouse, is are you gonna do anything about it?"

Newhouse, incredulous, found it hard to organize his thoughts into words. "Mr. Phillips, I am frankly astonished. I have felt from the start that this hearing was being conducted fairly and objectively. I have said so not once but more than once. I feel the answers to the questions, or rather lack of answers, can lead Mr. Kassel to only one conclusion. And again I advise you in your own best interests to respond quickly and honestly to questions asked you from now on. I will add one more thought. You are making it increasingly difficult for me to represent and defend you."

Phillips turned to the board and his eyes moved from man to man. There was not a sound in the room. "Well," he said, "I've got you guys against me, Kassel here against me, and now my own lawyer. Some deal, huh?"

The silence in the room continued.

Kassel, still calm, looked at Costello. "Should I continue?"

Costello, his patience clearly becoming thin, said, "If you have the strength."

"Thank you. One more question on this issue, Mr. Phillips, then we'll move on. Following your meeting with Mr. Gomez, he got a check in the mail. It was for $25. The name on the check was not known to Mr. Gomez. Mr. Gomez did not cash the check. I have it here in my hand. Did you have that check sent to Mr. Gomez?"

"No, I did not send it."

"I did not ask you that. Please answer the question, sir. Did you or did you not have that check sent?"

"I may have. I don't remember the amount. It was certainly not a check on any account of mine."

"I would think not, sir," said Kassel, sarcasm now clear in his voice.

"For the record, Mr. Phillips, and to dispose of this matter, we have traced the check. It was written by a member of your company's office staff, a man named Courtney Hames. The check was drawn on his personal account. Mr. Hames will, I'm sure, when faced with the specific question under oath, tell us that he wrote the check on orders from you. Do you want us to ask Mr. Hames that question, sir?"

"You stay the hell away from my employees, Kassel!"

"Thank you, Mr. Phillips, I'll take that as a `no.'"

Costello stood up. "Gentlemen, let's take a ten minute break."

At 9 P.M., Costello again called the meeting to order and turned the proceedings over to Kassel.

"Sir, we have statements from two other staff members that you made contact with them, asking them to meet with you for the purpose of getting information about various members of the board of governors. I ask you now if, after being directed not to contact staff people to have them give you confidential information, you did indeed continue to do so?"

"I'm not sure. I might have."

"I see, you might have. I'll take that as a `yes'. Kassel looked meaningfully at Newhouse, who shook his head.

"All right, Mr. Phillips, I'll end that line of questioning. We come now to the additional issues of your continued pursuit of charges against Mr. Branch, further, your continued pursuit of letters to the entire Club membership, in one of which you made specific charges against three board of governor members. Thus, some 875 men and women were exposed to the charges, none of which was substantiated by facts. You were asked to come to this hearing with such facts, proof of what you charged them with. My question is do you now have such proof?"

"I don't know. You've brought up several different points."

"Sir, I brought up one main point; that you made charges against three board members in letters to the entire membership. Let's not play games, Mr. Phillips. Do you have proof of your charges?"

"I didn't bring it with me."

"You mean you didn't bring any proof?"

"That's what I said."

"You were asked to do so, were you not? You told the membership you had proof of all your accusations. Was that true? Do you have proof?"

"I already told you I didn't bring it with me."

Kassel remained steady. "All right, sir, I will ask the secretary to make a ruling."

Costello, visibly tiring, said, "My ruling is that in the absence of any kind of proof, it appears obvious there is no such proof. The charges are unsubstantiated. Please proceed, Mr. Kassel."

"Let me now turn our attention to the letters to the membership. Those letters were clearly in opposition to the directive given you by the board. The letters are also against the spirit of the bylaws, which specify how member complaints are to be handled. Why did you write those letters, sir?"

"It's simple. I felt the board was not going to do anything about anything. I felt they were going to shove the whole matter under the damn rug."

"Did you consider the possible damage to the reputations of those people you accused?"

"It serves them right for what they did."

"But, sir, you have not established what they did. No proof of anything. Did you consider the damage you might be doing to the reputation of the Club itself?"

"Well, I felt that unless the whole mess was straightened out, the club would suffer far more serious damage. Everybody knows how I feel about this Club."

"How *do* you feel about the Club, sir?"

"I would do anything to keep the Club from going down the toilet, which is where it's going."

At this point one board member slapped his hand hard against the table top. He stood up, then sat down. "Son of a bitch," he said to no one in particular.

Costello was about to speak to the board member, then changed his mind. "Please, gentlemen, no more outbursts. Thank you."

Kassel continued. "Sir, did you send a copy of your letter to the various Club presidents in the area?"

"I might have. Yes, I guess I did."

Kassel, his eyes straight on Phillips, said, "We have sworn statements from the presidents of eight golf clubs in the area that you did indeed send them copies of the letters to members. What was your objective in doing that?"

"Oh, I don't know. I just thought they should know about it."

"I see. Did you give any thought to what it might do to the reputation of the Club?"

Phillips, now tiring himself, said, "By that time I thought the Club's reputation had already been badly damaged. Everyone in town knows that all kinds of bad stuff was going on here."

"I see. Did you also send a copy of the letters to the mayor of Bridgeside?"

"I don't remember. I may have, I don't know for sure."

"The mayor says you sent him a copy of the letters. Do you dispute that?"

"I guess not."

"I see. Mr. Phillips, I now come to the last of the issues. Did you send checks to two other Club employees, presumably in some kind of payment for information?"

"Please rephrase the question."

"All right. Did you send checks to Marianne Esterbrook?"

"I did not send checks to anyone."

"All right, I guess we've established that you *caused* checks to be sent. Did you *cause* checks to be sent to Ms. Esterbrook?"

"All right, I did. She performed a valuable service."

"To anyone else? Did you cause checks to be sent to anyone else?"

"One other person also performed a valuable service. I felt it was worth something."

"I have one last question, sir. In sending those checks, or rather having them sent, I ask you if you feel the spirit of Club policy was being violated?"

"The *spirit*?"

"Yes, Mr. Phillips, the spirit. It would seem that this kind of payment is hardly the kind of practice one would expect in a quality country club. At least that's my view. Is it yours?"

"Well, Mr. Attorney, you've asked a lot of questions tonight, and I don't much agree with anything you've said."

Kassel closed his file folder. "I see. Thank you, Mr. Phillips."

He turned to Costello. "Mr. Secretary, that concludes my questions."

Costello looked at his watch. It was almost 10 P.M.

Chapter Thirty

The Hearing Part II

At 10:15 P.M. Costello called the hearing back to order.

He spoke to both Phillips and Newhouse. "Gentlemen, the floor now belongs to you. There is no format for your remarks. You may direct your comments and questions to individuals or to the group. You will not be interrupted, and there is no time limit on you."

Newhouse, after a quick look at his client, stood up and began to speak. "Gentlemen, as you know, I am a late addition to this proceeding. I have only recently been retained by Mr. Phillips, and I have no long-range connection with him, nor do I have any background in the Pheasant Ridge Country Club. I know no members of the Club, nor am I familiar with its history and its policies. I have, of course, reviewed the bylaws of the Club, and I have researched, as thoroughly as time has permitted, the facts of this matter. I have read all the correspondence, and I believe I have a pretty firm grasp of most of it.

"Let me say at this point that I will do my very best to represent my client. That is my job. But let me also say this is a rather uncomfortable time for me. First, I am a young attorney with limited experience. Second, I am but a recent participant in this problem between the Club and Mr. Phillips. Third, I do not belong to a country club and I have no real feel for what goes on. Fourth and last, I thank you all for the courtesy and professionalism with which this hearing is being conducted. I personally appreciate it and I feel my client does too, although he can, of course, speak for himself.

"In total truth I cannot defend many of the actions of my client in this matter. I believe he has not always acted in good judgement. However, I would be less than a dedicated lawyer if I did not try as hard as I can to persuade you not to vote to dismiss Mr. Phillips from your Club.

"In that regard I would ask you to consider two very critical points. One, from the beginning, Mr. Phillips has done what he sincerely believed to be in the best interests of the Club. He believed, and still does, that the Club was being operated and managed in a way that was not suitable. He was trying to right what he considered to be a wrong. Several wrongs, in fact: An incompetent Club manager. A restaurant manager of doubtful values. What he perceived to be wrong-doing by the Club president and at least two of the board members. His tactics may be held by you to be objectionable. But his motives were pure.

"Now for the second point. It is a very key point and I ask you to consider it carefully. My research tells me, and it may not be complete, that in the history of the Club only six members have ever been expelled. That's six members in nearly eighty-five years! And in fact, the figure `six' may even be in error because two of the expulsions happened so long ago there is inadequate information about it.

"So for the purposes of my remarks, I am going on the assumption that the number is actually four. Just four members in all these many years. Thus it is a terribly strong move to cause a member to be expelled. The fact that only four members have been expelled in more than eighty-five years is an indication of the extreme seriousness. Previous boards, obviously, have treaded very carefully and cautiously on this issue.

"So let me briefly review for you the circumstances of the previous expulsions. One was made for drunkenness on the part of a member, repeated drunkenness and objectionable behavior in the Club area, in the restaurant areas, and on the golf course. He was warned time and again, and his offenses continued over a period of several years before the board acted.

"Another member was expelled for cheating on the golf course. He had been suspected for cheating frequently and was finally caught red-handed. This too went on for some time before the board acted.

"A third member was expelled, not only for repeated drunkenness but for totally unacceptable behavior. In one instance, for example, he unzipped his trousers and urinated in the Club grill. I will not go into further detail, but the expulsion was obviously carefully considered, and the board at that time even considered having the member go through counseling before they made their final decision to expel.

"The facts on the fourth member are obscure, very hard to come by. It appears he insulted a member's wife and may have hit the member with his fist. These may or may not be the real facts, but it's all I could determine. I believe we can all agree that each expulsion was appropriate. My client, on the other hand, does not drink, or, at worst, drinks only infrequently and limits hinself to a light beer at such times. Certainly he does not cheat on the golf course. And he has contributed mightily to the well-being of the Club over a period of many years. His actions in this matter do not come close to the behavior of the four other members who have been expelled.

"I acknowledge that his behavior has been less than exemplary. I acknowledge that he has at times conducted himself in a manner both objectionable and contrary to your wishes. However, it was all in complete sincerity and in the best interests of your Club."

Newhouse paused and let the point sink in. Costello, his attorney's viewpoint at work, conceded to himself it was an effective plea.

Newhouse again spoke. "I thank you for your courtesy and willingness to listen to a young lawyer getting his feet wet."

x x x x x x

Costello said, "Thank you, Mr. Newhouse. Now, Mr. Phillips, do you wish to speak?"

"Yes, I do." He stood up, holding a batch of papers in his hand. The half smile was again on his lips, but it was totally mirthless.

"You've heard my attorney, now you'll hear from me. I know that several of you do not like me. Fine. I don't like you either. But all I ask you to do is listen and be fair in your judgement of me. All I have ever wanted since this thing started was what is good for the Club. The Club is my life. Almost every non-business hour of my life has been devoted to this place. Some of you know I am not the greatest family man in the world, and for many years this Club has received far more attention from me than my family has. My son, in fact, told me I should drop all this business."

Phillips smiled as he said these words, and the room remained silent. Every board member was watching him intensely.

"Okay, you might not like me, but you know I care about this Club. No one can argue that point. From the very beginning I knew that your Claude Branch was a loser, not the kind of manager we needed. The man I personally recommended would have been far superior, I know that for a fact. Branch hired Russ Manders, or whatever the hell his name is. I suspected Manders from the beginning, too. I thought he was a fag. He had fag friends. One of them visited the Club one day. A queer is a queer and not good for anything, much less being the restaurant manager of one of the finest golf clubs in America.

"Queers attract people of their own kind, and down the road we'll see more and more of them. You've all heard my charges against Branch. I still think you got to the women he molested. But I can't do anything about that. I still think you got to Marianne Esterbrook and got her to shut up and not give me information, information I needed to make my case. And I think you got to that head engineer, the guy with the Mexican name.

"Everything I've tried to do in the best interests of the Club, you've built road blocks up to prevent me from acting. You've built a shield around what you're doing and you pay no attention to me, a longtime member and former president. It's pretty shoddy, guys. What I've tried to do is what many members would do if they had the guts. They're afraid to rock the boat. I've got the guts and I'm their spokesman. I represent the `silent majority.'

"Well, I've got nowhere with what I've tried to do about the poor management you've chosen. So now I'll address those members of this board I've accused of various wrongdoing. Mr. Ashley, do you remember when I came to you and said you'd made a mistake in hiring Branch?"

"Yes, I do," said Ashley, looking straight at Phillips.

"Do you remember what I said was my reason?"

"I remember you spoke against him. I remember you saying you did not like him. I remember you saying he was lazy. I do not remember any specifics or any reasons beyond your own dislike. Intense dislike, I might add."

"Okay, Chuck, have it your way. You're the big boss around here. I'm just a bystander." He looked at the other members, but no one smiled or spoke.

"Do you remember, Chuck, when I cautioned you against the kind of arrangement you were trying to make with the office about your bill?"

"I remember you didn't like it. You gave me no reason."

"Yes, I did. I told you it was cheating."

"Mr. Phillips, I won't dignify a response to that word. My arrangement on billing is the same one that has been in existence since I have been a member of this Club. Since the time when you, Mr. Phillips were the president, and on the board. It was done to simplify the account because there were several members of my family signing chits and there had been many mistakes. We had the account put under one number and all my family uses that number. No one has ever raised an objection to that procedure, not even you, when you were president!"

Phillips smiled the sardonic smile. "Well, I won't pursue it. You've got the board fooled on that one."

"Mr. Phillips," said Ashley, his face white and his voice filled with loathing, "I have responded to your point now and in the past. I deeply resent your use of the word `cheating' and I ask your attorney to take note of that. There is a limit, sir, to what I will take from you, and I am very close to that limit."

Phillips seemed about to ask another question related to the same point, but, noting Ashley's extreme anger, thought better of it.

He shrugged. "All right, I'll get off that one. But I still think what I think. Now I want to ask Parsons a question. Parsons, did you hire a decorator for the remodeling project without approval of the membership?"

Parsons was calm in his response. "First, Mr. Phillips, I did not hire the decorator. That decision was a committee decision. The majority ruled. In fact, I was in favor of another person. But for your information, membership approval is not required for the hiring of decorators, construction companies, or other contractors. Having been president, you surely know that."

Phillips said, "Did you know the decorator was a fag?"

Coldly, Parsons said, "First of all, I did not ask the man's sexual orientation. That has nothing to do with his competence. Only one on our committee raised that as an issue. It did not come up again and thank God, it did not! Second, and although I am not naive, I resent your use of the word `fag.' It does you no credit, and it clearly does not belong in the context of this hearing."

Phillips sneered, "Well, we'll have to see about that. Okay, let me ask you this. Did you accept a free round of drinks because of your House Committee membership or because of your board membership?"

Parsons, his voice rising slightly, said, "First, sir, I accepted no free round of drinks for any service I performed for this Club. Second, you may be referring to a chit I signed after a board meeting golf outing. As soon as I signed the chit, the president told me that the chit was invalid, that board members are not required to pay for refreshment during the afternoon and evening of a board meeting golf outing. The president crossed the chit out and called it to the attention of the Club manager. Third, this also happened in the case of two other board meetings for the same purpose. I was new to the board at that time, and I signed the chit without knowing that in such a circumstance refreshments were on the Club."

Phillips said, "Well, it's nice you guys have all these little perks to benefit you."

Parsons felt his stomach muscles tense, and he was about to reply when Costello spoke. "I must jump in here. Because I was sure this issue would come up, I have checked past presidents on the subject. Of the seven past presidents I spoke to, all said that the policy of gratis refreshment during and because of board meetings had been in place for many years. Board members work hard and give freely of their time, and little perks like this are small reward for such work. I will also add, Mr. Phillips, that this policy was in effect when you were president of this Club."

Phillips did not respond immediately. Then he said, "I see you've done some checking. I didn't know about such a policy, and I think anyone taking advantage of it is scum of the earth."

Costello was unable to restrain himself. "Mr. Phillips, you are out of order. At this point, and as a control factor in this meeting, I warn you against derogatory remarks about any individual on our board. Such remarks will simply not be permitted. We are supposed to all be gentlemen here. Mr. Newhouse, you are so advised, as are you, Mr. Phillips."

Phillips shrugged his shoulders again, a maneuver that was now familiar. He said, "Well, I'm about done. I won't go any further on this. However, I do want to say this. I love this Club, it is my life, and I don't want to be expelled. I want to continue to serve the Club as I have in the past. I would like to feel that all my many contributions over many years are worth something now. If you want me to get on my knees and kiss all your asses, I'll do that."

"That will not be necessary, Mr. Phillips. Do I understand that you have concluded your remarks?"

"Yes, sir," said Phillips.

"Gentlemen," said Costello, with a weary sigh. "It is now 11:15 P.M. Does anyone have a comment or question?"

"I do, Mr. Secretary," said Parsons. "Not that it's necessary, but I'd like to clear up the issue of the supposed homosexuality of Mr. Russell Manders. I very much dislike doing this, but I hate to see any kind of cloud hanging over anyone, particularly a man—and I emphasize the word `man'—who has performed so well for this Club and its members. I know Mr. Manders very well, I have met his fiance and members of his family. For your information Mr. Manders has a brother who is gay, and this brother has applied here for a job in the restaurant area. He is a fine young man, and I have personally interviewed him. I would not hesitate to hire him. However, Mr. Manders, sensitive to the issue, told me that his brother was withdrawing his application. He did not wish to cause any kind of problem. I hope that clears up this point, and again I apologize to the enlightened men in this room for having to air such a disagreeable subject."

"Thank you, Frank. Anyone else? No? All right, I declare this hearing at an end. Mr. Phillips and Mr. Newhouse, you are now free to go. Thank you."

Phillips and Newhouse rose from the table and left the room.

Chapter Thirty-one

The Vote

The remaining men around the table, all of them weary and some angry at Phillips's parting remarks, waited for Costello to continue the hearing. There was very little conversation.

Costello directed a question at Ashley. "Chuck, I will now turn the hearing over to you, as president of the club, and we can proceed as you wish."

Ashley shook his head. "No, Larry, I want to remain as a kind of bystander. I'd like you to continue, if that's all right with you."

Costello grinned. "Thanks a lot. Okay gentlemen, what is your pleasure? It's late and we can gather again tomorrow night for discussion and the vote. Or we can stay here until we finish the job." He looked inquiringly around the table.

There were several comments, but the sense of the responses indicated the members were willing to stay and were willing to vote when the time came.

Costello said, "All right, we'll move on. I don't have any fancy ideas about what the procedure should be. I'm as new at this as you are. But I think we ought to have some discussion, then vote. okay? Anyone want to start?"

One member said, "I don't have a speech. I was impressed with the final remarks of that guy Newhouse. Very smart of him. He made some good points. But what Chet Phillips did went far beyond what any rational person would or should do. I've thought hard about it and I'm ready to vote."

Another member said, "No matter what the lawyer said, the question I have is how anyone can justify Phillips's actions as `in the best interests of the Club.' Fact is, he damn near wrecked this Club. He did it deliberately. And his motivation was only his own ego and desire to control. We've got to act decisively and not at the last minute start to get all weepy. Phillips is a detriment to this Club, a cancer."

There was silence for a moment, then another man spoke up. "If Phillips was thinking of the Club only, then there is a way he could have proceeded, a way to at least try to get done what he wanted done. He refused to follow the rules. He taunted the board and he banked on some kind of popularity within the membership to support him. I never felt any ground swell of support for him. Never. I'm ready to vote."

Still another man raised his hand. "Where Phillips lost me is when he constantly could not remember doing something we all know he did. And the other thing is that martyr role he tries to play. It makes me sick."

"Let's not let ourselves be like that O.J. Simpson jury, guys," this from one of the most consistently silent members of the board. "Those gutless wonders acquitted him when it was so very clear he was guilty. Probably the most shameful act in American legal history. Chet Phillips is guilty of breaking every rule we have in this Club. If we waver, if we let him off the hook, we're not serving the Club, and serving the Club is what we're here for."

Another member spoke. "I have no doubt what the right thing to do, is. But I'd like to ask Mr. Kassel a question. Dick, what is the likelihood, in your opinion, of Phillips suing this Club? And what do you think his chances would be?"

Kassel smiled. "Your guess is as good as mine as to whether he'd sue. But I'll say this. If he sues, I'd love to be the attorney on the other side."

Parsons said, "I don't think we ought to even entertain for a second what Phillips might do. We ought to vote for what we think is right."

There were several nods from the men at the table.

Costello said, "Gentlemen, I'm willing to stay here all night if you wish to continue the discussion. What is your wish?"

"I think we should vote," said one man, and the members all nodded their agreement.

"All right," said Costello. "The bylaws don't say what kind of vote it should be, so I'll make my own ruling. All those in favor of not expelling Mr. Phillips, raise their hands."

Not a hand went up.

"All right, all those in favor of expelling Chester Phillips from membership in Pheasant Ridge, raise their hands."

All hands but one, that of Charles Ashley, went up. "Remember, guys, I recused myself from the vote."

Costello said, "All right. Mr. Phillips has been unanimously voted out of the Club. I will inform him of this tomorrow morning. Unless there is any more discussion, I declare this hearing concluded. Thank you for your attendance and your patience. Oh, and for the record, our recorder should note that the vote was taken with Mr. Ashley recusing himself and one board member absent."

The woman said, "Yes, sir, I will note that point."

"Thank you," said Costello, "and thank you for your patience and professionalism."

It was eleven minutes to midnight.

x x x x x x

At 9:04 the morning of August 8, Costello called Phillips at his office. "Mr. Phillips, Chet, this is Larry Costello. You wanted to hear the result of the vote. The board voted to expel you from Pheasant Ridge. I will confirm this in writing, but I knew you wanted to hear without delay. The letter will specify the fact that this expulsion is for life. You cannot reapply at a later date. Do you have any questions?"

"Yes, I do, what was the vote? I mean how many for and how many against?"

"Chet, it was unanimous. One board member was not present, as you know, and Chuck Ashley recused himself for reasons that we can agree are obvious."

"You mean I can't ever get back in the Club? Ever? How long has that rule been in effect? Since last night?"

"Sir, expulsion, as I said, is for life. That policy has been in effect since the Club began. It appears on page 18. It has always been in effect. Always."

x x x x x x

At 10:15 P.M. the night of September 2, Cory Phillips, age twenty-eight, went into the garage at his home, got into his car, and started it. He did not open the garage doors. His body was discovered by a neighbor around noon the next day.

On September 6, Ashley and eight members of the Pheasant Ridge Board attended Cory Phillips's funeral services. Chester Phillips was not present.

EPILOGUE

On October 2 a bill for $93,000 came from the law offices of Richard Kassel. There was also a bill from the security man present at the hearing for $500. A bill from the recorder at the hearing for $450. A bill from the recorder at the earlier hearing, for $395.

*****

During the week of October 8, Ashley and Parsons played a nassau with Costello and another board member. Ashley and Parsons lost $3.

*****

In late October, Chester Phillips settled out of court with Claude Branch. The exact amount of the settlement was not disclosed, but someone close to the matter said it was in excess of $800,000.

*****

The suit by Russell Manders is not yet settled.

*****

In October, one of the two newspapers in the city published a two-page article on country clubs in the area. The article devoted 11 column inches to the Pheasant Ridge situation. The sub-headline of the story was: "Millionaire Country Club Members Wrangle, and Law-suits Abound." No one knows where the newspaper got its information.

*****

By late October, Chester Phillips had applied for membership in four different golf clubs in the area. All four turned him down.

*****

Also in October Branch landed on his feet at a fine club in Philadelphia, the site of several major golf tournaments over the years.

*****

In November the board unanimously agreed that Russell Manders would be the new general manager of Pheasant Ridge. At this time Manders dropped his suit against Phillips.

*****

In mid-December Marianne Esterbrook was discharged as comptroller of the Club, as of the end of the year.

*****

Chief engineer Bill Gomez was voted employee of the year at Pheasant Ridge. The honor included a bonus of $1,500.

*****

In January the board approached the membership with a plan for a total upgrading of the clubhouse. The plan was disapproved.

*****

In February attorney Kassel won a sexual harassment suit for a client prominent in the news. In news stories about the trial, Kassel was described as "one of the leading legal minds in the state."

Finale

The Complainers

"Jeez, I heard the legal bill to the Club for the Phillips's thing was $200 grand!"

"I heard it was more than that."

"My God, them lawyers!"

"D'ya think Phillips deserved to be kicked out?"

"I don't know. The board just wanted to show their power."

"I don't know about that, Chet sure as hell went bonkers. They had to do something."

"Did I tell you, I'm having my garage made bigger? Damn thing is gonna cost me four times what the damn house cost."

"Hell, that's nothing, I just paid $500 for a sport coat for my kid. I remember my first sport coat. Cost my old man $35."

"I hear the Club is going after the U.S. Open in a few years."

"Where'd you hear it was the Open? It's the PGA."

"Christ, why the hell are they doing that? The damn golf course will be ruined for two years!"

"Shit, guys, it isn't the Open and it isn't the PGA, it's some damn women's tournament."

"Well, anyway, we haven't got the parking, and there'll be women all over the damn place. And then all the wives will want open tee-times!"

"The damn board doesn't care about the members of this Club."

"Yeah, I heard they're gonna raise the dues again, at least 40 percent."

"Didjas hear they're gonna level the 9th green, take the hill out of it?"

"No shit?"

"My wife wants to redecorate our damn house. The estimate is three times what I paid for the house originally."

"No shit?"

"What d'ya think about Manders being made manager?"

"I hear he's queer."

"No, it's his brother."

"Same thing."

"I just got the bill for my wrist surgery. Fifteen grand, and that's just the beginning."

"My God, them doctors. I was in my doctor's office for just five minutes and the damn bill was $400."

"Did I tell you what my wife paid for a pound of hamburger the other day? A few years ago I coulda bought a T-bone steak for that."